Mazargues

A Jacques Forêt Mystery

Angela Wren

www.darkstroke.com

Copyright © 2022 by Angela Wren
Photography: Adobe Stock © Tomasz Zajda
Cover Design: Services for Authors
Editor: Sue Barnard
All rights reserved.

No part of this book may be used or reproduced in any manner whatsoever without written permission of the author or Crooked Cat except for brief quotations used for promotion or in reviews.
This is a work of fiction.
Names, characters, and incidents are used fictitiously.

First Dark edition, darkstroke, Crooked Cat Books. 2022

Discover us online:
www.darkstroke.com

Join us on facebook:
www.facebook.com/groups/darkstroke

Tweet a photo of yourself holding
this book to **@darkstrokedark**
and something nice will happen.

For Brian and Maggie, friends and fellow travellers in France.

Acknowledgments

My very grateful thanks go to:

Rachel, friend, art historian and lecturer

My local writing colleagues who can be relied upon to comment, encourage and to answer my many questions,

My editor and publisher, without whom none of the books in this series would have been possible, for taking a chance on me,

Readers for selecting my books and reviewers for their most valuable comments.

About the Author

Angela Wren is an actor and director at a small theatre a few miles from where she lives in the county of Yorkshire in the UK. She worked as a project and business change manager – very pressured and very demanding – but she managed to escape, and now she writes books.

She has always loved stories and story-telling, so it seemed a natural progression, to her, to try her hand at writing, starting with short stories. Her first published story was in an anthology, which was put together by the magazine 'Ireland's Own' in 2011.

Angela particularly enjoys the challenge of plotting and planning different genres of work. Her short stories vary between contemporary romance, memoir, mystery, and historical. She also writes comic flash-fiction and has drafted two one-act plays that have been recorded for local radio.

Her full-length stories are set in France, where she likes to spend as much time as possible each year.

Follow Angela at **www.angelawren.co.uk** and
www.jamesetmoi.blogspot.co.uk

The Jaques Forêt Mystery series by Angela Wren:

Messandrierre (#1)
Merle (#2)
Montbel (#3)
Marseille (#4)
Mercœur (#5)
Mazargues (#6)

Mazargues

A Jacques Forêt Mystery

le faubourg de mazargues dans le 9e

A broad shaft of moonlight silvered the dead-end of boulevard des Anges, reaching just under the leaves of a large shrub growing beneath the high canopy of a two-hundred-year-old *platane*. The edge of the pale light was reflected in the green irises of a pair of staring and wide-open, but unseeing, eyes. For a few seconds, the face was lit with an eerie iridescence.

    A whisper of warm southern wind gently played through a thin shank of copper-coloured hair that had fallen across the pallid and rigid visage. The strand lifted and then fell in response to the sea breeze. The momentary current silently dissipated to nothing as the balmy air of the night settled. A heavy bank of cloud rolled across the moon, obliterating any remaining brightness, returning the narrow corner to its previous darkness: a deep shadow sufficient to obscure the pool of crimson that had formed on the once-white clothing of the body that lay there.

the suburb of mazargues in the 9th,
may 1st, 2019, 23.58

col de la tourette, wednesday, may 29th, 2019, 16.17

Jacques paced across the *aire* for the fourth time. Having arrived promptly for the appointed meeting at four, he was happy to wait out the few intervening minutes in the brightness of the afternoon sunshine. His irritation had begun to increase once his watch registered ten minutes past the hour. Rechecking the time, he clenched his jaw. *Eighteen minutes late.* He always made a point of being on time and disliked being kept waiting.

"Do I wait, or do I leave?" He turned full circle. The forest trail to his right was empty, there was no access from the valley behind and the main road that ran from St Étienne to Mende was moderately quiet. He glanced at the switchback junction with the minor road to Bleymard opposite. *Will she come by car? If so, from which direction?* His lack of information was beginning to frustrate him. But the caller had made certain that she could not be contacted.

Deciding to wait longer, he retraced his steps and halted in front of the upright stone at one side of the small parking area. Although he'd driven past the memorial on many occasions, he had never once stopped to look at it. His gaze followed the words of the short introductory phrase. The next line was a date, and he stared at it: *le 29 mai, 1944.*

"Does my being here have something to do with what happened more than sixty years ago?" He muttered to himself and immediately shook the idea from his mind whilst continuing to read about the deaths of those fighting for his country's freedom during the Occupation.

"Monsieur Forêt?"

Jacques spun around. In front of him was a small, slightly-built woman. Little more than a metre and a half tall, he reckoned.

"*Enchanté*, Madame," he said, offering her his hand.

Moving her Nordic walking stick to her left hand, she pulled off her glove with her teeth and then took his. Jacques was surprised to find that her grip was firm.

He turned to the stone. "Is this why you insisted on meeting me here?"

"No. The massacre that this memorial commemorates is of historic importance, but this place is always quiet and usually empty. Shall we move over here?" She took a few steps away from the edge of the road towards the wooden fence that marked the boundary of the parking area.

Jacques nodded and followed her lead.

"There must be no possibility that we can be overheard, Monsieur Forêt. That's why I chose this location." She pulled a small canvas rucksack off her back and dropped it to the ground. "No one can come up behind us here," she said as she looked across the deep, green and heavily-wooded valley below the col. She turned around and leaned against the log fence. "And if anyone pulls in, we will see them immediately and stop talking."

Jacques rested his left foot on the bottom rung of the fence and zipped up the top of his leathers a little. The sun was warm, but the mountain breeze was from the northwest and still held the remnants of an early spring chill.

"You're not quite what I expected," she said.

He glanced down at her. "In what way, Madame?"

"The leathers. That bike. I presume it is yours."

Jacques glanced over to the sixty-year-old machine and smiled. It had taken a lot of time and effort to get it back to its current gleaming and fully-working condition. The gold and silver metal of the framework and wheels shimmered in the bright sunlight. It was an indulgence. He knew that. But it had been a great solace in the dark times. And there had been too many hours of solitary darkness over the last five years.

The weather for the long weekend was forecast to be good, and that had been the sole deciding factor in his mode of transport that morning. The schools were closing that day for the religious festival, and having his son Lucien at home was an excellent reason for his decision to take the day after *Jour de l'Ascension* as a holiday.

"Yes, it's mine," he said, turning to face her. "And I've spent far too long restoring it."

"Impressive." She grinned at him and nodded.

Jacques was keen to move the conversation around to why he had been summoned. "In the telephone messages you left for me, you said you had some work that might be of interest. So, why am I here, Madame?"

"I want you to find a painting for me."

Jacques stared at the dark-grey tarmac of the road. The request was not what he had expected. He wondered if it was genuine. He also wasn't sure why she had chosen him for the task. Yet, she had faced him as she had spoken the words.

"Madame, I will not undertake any work that is not legal. If you are thinking that I can—"

"No! Not at all, Monsieur. I want you to recover what is legally mine. That is all." She pulled off her bush hat and scrubbed her fingers through her thick white hair. The sunlight playing on the close-cropped locks made the colourless strands shimmer, providing greater contrast between the sheen of her hair and the sun-browned skin of her face.

Jacques thought for a moment. Art theft was big business amongst a particular sector of the criminal classes. He'd come up against a couple of burglars who stole art and antiques on demand whilst he had been a serving detective in Paris. *But here? Art theft here in Mende?* The idea just didn't fit with his limited and acquired knowledge of the trade. But there was a market, he had to admit that. A strong and thriving underground market for artworks of all kinds.

"If the picture has been stolen, why have you not informed the police?" Jacques watched her reaction closely. He also hoped that she would remove her oversized sunglasses. If he could see her eyes, he could be more definite about whether or not she was speaking the truth.

The woman turned away. "I guessed that was what you

would think," she said, facing him again, the bright sunlight distracting and reflecting in the dark tint of the lenses of her shades. "I suppose, technically, it has been stolen."

Jacques felt he was losing his grip on the conversation. He stared across the parking area at a large logging truck striving to make it up to the top of the incline.

"Technically?" Jacques shrugged. "It's quite simple, Madame. Either you have the painting, or you don't. If you don't, then it must have been stolen, sold, gifted to someone else or destroyed. In the last three instances, there would be no need for me to be here because you would have knowledge of the disposal of your artwork."

The woman grinned. "Yes, you're right. And no, the painting hasn't been sold or given away. Well, not by me, anyway. As for it being destroyed, I sincerely hope not."

Jacques frowned as he thought through the implications of her last statement. "Might it have been sold or given away by someone else? And might that other person, somehow, be instrumental in the theft or disappearance?"

The woman smiled. "Monsieur Forêt, please, just find my painting. That is all I want. Its return. I don't want any police involvement because that will make everything public. The art market is very fickle, and I can't afford any form of taint to be attached to my picture. I just want my piece of art back. And I know you can do it, Monsieur. You found the opera singer's son in a few days. It was all over the newspapers. That's why I—"

A car pulled into the *aire*. Jacques and the woman fell silent and watched as a young mother got out of the vehicle, ran to the passenger door and opened it. A few moments later she was shepherding a small boy to the other side of the door, remonstrating with him as she did so. Jacques smiled. He'd stopped counting the number of times his son had decided he needed to relieve himself whilst on a journey. Lucien was a little older now, and such impromptu stops had finally become a thing of the past. At least that was what he hoped.

"I will give consideration to taking your case, Madame, but first I must have all of the facts," he said, without thinking about any possible consequences. *We need this work.*

The young mother bundled her boy into the car and was back behind the wheel in a moment. She set off at such speed that the back tyres left a swirling cloud of dust in their wake. Jacques glanced at the stone and couldn't help wondering about the appropriateness of the driver's use of the space.

"You'll need this," said the woman, pulling a large brown envelope out of her rucksack. "There's a printed picture of my painting in there. I must insist on discretion at all times, Monsieur Forêt." She shouldered her bag and then pulled on her hat.

"Of course." He folded the envelope in half and tucked it into the inside pocket of his leathers. When he looked up, the woman was striding away. Her tread was assured and brisk.

"I'll be in touch first thing next week, and I'll be ringing you for daily updates," she shouted without looking back.

Jacques slumped against the fence. When he looked in the direction the woman had taken, he realised she had slipped out of his field of vision and onto one of the forest paths. He thought about trying to follow her, but changed his mind.

"I think she may be very fit, and I suspect she will know those routes much better than I do." He fastened the collar stud on his leathers and meandered across to the bike. His holiday weekend was about to begin, and Marie Mancelle, a near neighbour always willing to help out with childcare, would be wondering when he would be picking up his son.

Jacques sat astride the bike and considered what this new case might bring. Assuming he accepted the commission, he mentally reminded himself. He put on his helmet. A few moments later, he pulled out into the stream of traffic that was heading north from the city of Mende. Everyone who was able to would be taking Friday as a non-working day to be with family, and Jacques was looking forward to a few days away from the office. As he rounded the sweeping bend, he notched up his speed. He moved past the cars and powered along the RN88 towards Messandrierre.

messandrierre, wednesday, may 29th, 21.08

Jacques sat alone in the loft overlooking the small front garden of the chalet. Wednesday was Gaston's usual evening for closing the bar early and coming across for a beer or two and some conversation on the odd occasion when Jacques was in the village during the week. It had been almost a month since the two of them had sat debating the world's issues once Lucien was in bed. As the next day was a public holiday, Jacques felt sure his old friend would continue working. The opportunity to make a few extra euros before the weekend was too good to miss.

A light contented breath emanated from the baby monitor. Jacques smiled as he lifted his attention from the financial papers in his hands. He counted to himself as he listened for the next exhalation.

"Five seconds. Always five." He glanced at the battered and not-so-sparkling-white little device on the coffee table as though it might respond. "I really should get rid of that," he told himself for the thousandth time, only to find the same arguments and counter-arguments jostling through his mind. He dismissed the thoughts and the inevitable conclusion to keep the monitor just a while longer.

He took another look at the spreadsheet and focussed his mind. The business had been barely breaking even for the last nine months or so. His colleague, Didier Duclos, was coming to the end of a month's unpaid leave, and Thibault Clergue had been laid off since the beginning of March. What little work there had been, Jacques had handled almost entirely alone. It seemed that even divorce cases – an area of work he considered the bread-and-butter of private investigation – were becoming rare.

"We can't carry on like this," he muttered. He put the

spreadsheet face-down on the table. It wasn't that he wanted to deny the parlous state of the business finances. He knew he couldn't do that. He just needed to take a little respite from the glaring contrasts between the black and the red numbers in front of him.

He stared at the still-unopened brown envelope he'd acquired that afternoon. *Does the answer really lie there?* The silence, and the realisation that a case about a missing painting might bring a great deal of work for little reward, did nothing to lift his spirits.

Grabbing the envelope, he ripped it open and let the meagre contents fall onto the table. He sifted through them and arranged everything so he could see each item. Not that there was a lot to examine: a page taken from a magazine or booklet containing an illustration of a painting, some information printed from the internet, and a cutting from an old newspaper. Jacques pulled the envelope apart, checking that no other items were still clinging to the interior. He systematically looked at everything to see if there were any contact details or clues about the person who was commissioning the case. Nothing.

"How am I supposed to contact you, Madame, if you don't give me a name or phone number?" Reaching to pull his phone from his pocket, he changed his mind. He knew there was no point. In response to the first two messages left on his mobile, he had tried to call the originating number, but the connection had failed in each case. Even a text in response to the second message, requesting more details, had not been delivered. When asked to check the numbers, his colleague Maxim had discovered that each one was unobtainable and untraceable. "Probably burner phones," Maxim had said. When the third message arrived, Jacques knew he would have to be at the appointed place on the designated day and on time, whether he wanted to be there or not.

He glanced at the items on the table. *No contact details. No opportunity for questions or debate.* He pinched the bridge of his nose and let out a heavy sigh.

"And what do I know about art?" He lolled back on the

sofa. "Nothing," he said in answer to his own question. "I know nothing about art." He glanced at the newspaper article. *And if I'm going to take this case, I need to learn fast.* Holding on to the thought, he stood.

The bang as the small front gate clapped shut drew his attention to the garden below, where he saw Gaston striding towards the chalet. Jacques scrabbled everything together, including the monitor, and quickly sprinted down the spiral staircase. He waved to Gaston as he stood in the front doorway waiting for his friend.

"I hope you've got that good bottle of single malt out for me," said Gaston as he climbed the steps onto the porch.

Jacques grinned and nodded. "I sense something is amiss," he said as he stood aside.

"Stephanie is pregnant!" Gaston stomped through to the snug and collapsed down on the sofa.

Jacques closed the front door and followed him through. "But, that's good news, isn't it?" He dropped the bundle of papers and the monitor onto the low table in front of the settee.

Gaston shook his head. "Do you really know my son-in-law?"

Jacques collected a couple of glasses and a bottle from a shelf at the top of the bookcase. He'd decided a few months ago that convenience was more important than tidying everything away in kitchen cupboards out of Lucien's vision. Keeping things out of his son's reach had become enough.

"Probably not," said Jacques as he placed a glass in front of his companion.

"He may be a posh *notaire* in his father's practice in Clermont, but he is a fool."

Jacques frowned. "He can't be that stupid if he's got his legal qualifications." Sensing his friend needed it, he poured a good measure of whisky into Gaston's glass.

"He might have letters after his name, Jacques, but there's barely a grain of common sense or practicality anywhere in his head."

"Alright." Jacques added a small measure of malt to his

glass and sank into his favourite armchair. "I think that's a bit harsh, Gaston. He seemed like a decent man when I met him at the wedding, and I thought—"

"Ha! The wedding! And can you imagine what the christening is going to be like?" Gaston took a large gulp from his glass.

Jacques let out a quiet snort of laughter. "So that's what's upsetting you, is it?"

"I've already told Marianne that I'm not going to the christening if I have to dress up like a clown!"

Jacques grinned. "You said the same about the wedding, but you were still there." He took a sip of his drink. "And, as Marianne said to me then, you'll do anything for your daughter. And what is so wrong with having a proper haircut and wearing a smart and fashionable suit once in a while?" Jacques glanced at Gaston's usual garb: faded jeans, a checked open-neck shirt and loafers. It seemed Gaston had been born in those clothes.

"It feels uncomfortable, Jacques. I'm really happy in my ageing-hippy skin."

"Gaston, you are barely five years older than me, and hippies were has-beens before you even made it to the *lycée*."

Gaston sniffed in disapproval and knocked back the remainder of his drink.

"I suppose I should say congratulations; you're going to be a *grand-père*. Something to be celebrated."

Gaston smoothed his thumb and forefinger across his drooping grey moustache. "Don't remind me," he said. "It's too sobering a thought." He reached for the bottle and poured himself another drink. "Marianne's already making plans for visits and time away to be with Stephanie and the baby when it comes."

Jacques winced at his friend's insensitivity. "He or She will be your grandchild, Gaston. The future for your family. You can't change that."

Gaston slumped back in his seat. "I know," he said, cradling his glass. "I just thought I, we, would have a bit more time for ourselves before the next generation came along." Gaston stared at Jacques. "I was hoping for a little more sympathy, too."

"Sorry, but the whisky is the only sympathy you'll get. I've got a few issues of my own to deal with. But, *santé*." Jacques raised his tumbler in tribute to Stephanie and her husband, and took a sip.

Gaston plonked his glass on the table. "Thanks, but I'll go." He stood up and started to move away.

"No! Gaston, that's not what I meant. Just sit down, finish your drink and give yourself time to get used to the idea. A new baby in the family is a good thing."

A deep frown appeared on Gaston's forehead. "I know," he said, sitting down again. "But they've only been married eleven months, and a first baby puts such a serious strain on a relationship."

Jacques didn't need to be reminded of that truth. The worry, the sleepless nights, the constant visits to the hospital, and then the… All the memories came flooding back and slammed into his conscious mind like a vast, black wrecking ball. Refusing to let his sadness get the upper hand, he kept his thoughts to himself, picked up the bottle and added a small splash of the amber liquid to his drink.

"She's not my little girl any more, is she?" Gaston shook his head and gently swilled the malt around in his glass.

"Stephanie hasn't been your little girl for a long time, Gaston. Just like her *papa*, she can take care of herself. I've known that ever since I first met her. If she feels now is the right time for her family to grow, then you should be happy for her. Stop wallowing!"

Gaston took a slug of the whisky. "I should've known not to come. You're lucky. Boys are easier to manage than girls."

Jacques let out a gasp. "And how would you know that? You only have one daughter!"

Gaston stood. "I need a smoke," he said, pulling his packet of Gitanes from his jeans pocket. "I'll be outside."

Jacques nodded.

Gaston lumbered out of the room as though he had the weight of the world on his shoulders. *I just hope you will have come to your senses by the time you get to the end of that cigarette.*

Comfortable in his armchair, Jacques separated the various bits of paper. The page with the picture of the painting on it was the only item that immediately caught his attention. A scene on a beach. The grey-blue of the sea reaching across the space enclosed only by the edges of the paper. The shifting shades of azure for the sky melding into the line of the horizon where it met the ocean. In the distance on the right, in slightly lighter grey hues spotted with misty patches of green, stood some cliffs and a line of land. In the foreground, an expanse of soft, dry, golden sand and some figures.

"One side of a very large bay. I wonder where that is?"

Jacques turned the page over. On the back was a single column of text in English to the right of the page. In the bottom left-hand corner, in smaller print, was an arrow pointing right, and a note which read:

Child in the Park, ca. 1889
Oil on panel: 10⅞ x 7¼ in. (27.6 x 18.4 cm)
Signed: WM-C (1.1)
Inscription verso: ...sunlight on stone

Private collection

Exhibitions: **ExIENA '29 #130** as *Sunlight on Stone*

Jacques looked in the direction the arrow was pointing. The space to the right was where the missing page should have been. Even though it was obvious that the notes did not refer to the painting he had been asked to find, he was curious to know what the picture of the printed description looked like. He turned back to the beach scene.

"So, no title and no artist, unless..." He pulled the page closer to look for a signature. As his gaze shifted from one corner of the picture to the next, his attention was captured by the first of the figures. He studiously examined the child and then each of the four carefully-spaced groups, his original purpose lost in the detail. The individuals' clothes indicated that the scene was set around a hundred years earlier.

"Perhaps a little more," Jacques said to himself.

"More what?" Gaston stepped into the room, bringing with him the whiff of nicotine, and took his previous place on the sofa. "Art, Jacques? When did you become interested in art?"

"I'm not really," he said, dropping the page onto the table. "But I might have to take an interest soon if I'm to investigate this next case." He grabbed his glass and took a sip.

"If? I thought you said a few weeks ago that the finances were down the drain at the moment. You'll need any case you can get, won't you?"

Jacques wrinkled up his nose. "Ah, you know how it is with business," he said, holding his right hand out flat and tipping it left and right like a banking plane. "*Comme-çi, comme-ça.*"

Gaston nodded. "And this next case? If it concerns art, won't that involve a lot of money?"

"It might, had we been asked to provide a security detail. But it's just a search and find. That's a lot of work and not much return." Jacques shrugged.

"Would a revision of your pricing structure help?" Gaston sat forward, his elbows resting on his thighs with his fingers interlocked around his glass, wearing an earnest expression on his face.

Jacques grinned. He recognised the pose as that particularly favoured by his long-time friend when the possibility seemed likely of getting into a serious debate about business. Especially if the business under discussion was not Gaston's own.

"It's alright, Gaston – you can relax. Work has been a bit thin, but we're not about to go under yet. I just need to be careful for a little longer and let our latest drive to get new cases come to fruition."

Gaston emptied his glass. "I'd better be getting back," he said as he glanced at his watch. "Will you be at the *kermesse* on Sunday?"

Jacques nodded. "It's one of the reasons I brought the bike

with me."

Gaston stood up. "The Goldflash? You've finally got it finished?"

Jacques collected the glasses and replaced the cork in the bottle. "Yes. It's in the garage." He walked out of the snug, into the main living space and across to the kitchen.

"Take a look," he said, nodding to the door that led to the boot room and thence through to the garage. Gaston didn't hesitate. Jacques rinsed the glasses under the tap and then placed them in the top tray of the dishwasher. As he made his way through the obstacle course that was Lucien's idea of storing his shoes and trainers neatly, Jacques could hear a long low whistle coming from the garage. When he reached the doorway, he saw Gaston sitting astride the bike.

"Nice machine, Jacques. Very nice." He got off and stepped away. "And in the sunlight, I bet it shines."

"It does, and Lucien has made me promise to take him for a ride before anyone else." Jacques, his hands in the pockets of his jeans as he leaned against the doorjamb, stared at the motorbike. An overwhelming sense of well-being crept over him, and he took a deep breath.

Gaston frowned. "Lucien riding pillion. Is that legal, Jacques?"

"He's over the minimum age, but it isn't something I would normally do until he was much older. But on Sunday morning, the roads here will be very quiet. It's a down incline to the restaurant car park, if the engine isn't running and I'm wheeling the bike…" He shrugged.

"The downslope will help with the weight of the machine," said Gaston. "That boy of yours is one lucky lad. Add me to your list of guest passengers, and I'd better get back." As he drew level with Jacques, he nodded and placed his hand on his friend's shoulder. "Well done, and it's good to see it finished at last."

Jacques closed the door between the boot room and the garage, locked it, and followed his guest to the front door.

"I'll see you on Sunday," said Gaston. He stepped onto the porch and turned. "And if you want to know about art, ask

Père Chastain. He knows about paintings and has lots of books. I think he may have studied art and history, or something like that, before entering the seminary."

boulevard mont-rose, saturday, may 4th, 18.07

The narrow street stretched all along the coast from Marseille to the other side of Cap Croisette, which sat within the boundary of the Parc National des Calanques. The road had various names along its substantial length, but at the edge of the park, it became boulevard Mont-Rose.

The last house on the boulevard was set into the stone of the hillside, and a little further back than the rest of the properties. The misalignment was of great interest to the current owner, as it allowed uninterrupted views of the Mediterranean Sea.

The property had been in a dilapidated state when Milo had bought it. For cash. But after five years of substantial refurbishment and extension, the house became a home. A place to relax, somewhere to entertain business associates, and a retreat when he needed to lie low.

The lower floor of the original hillside residence had been opened out. All the small rooms had disappeared, and the resultant space had been flooded with light. A new wine cellar had been created, and occupied one section in the new extension on the eastern side of the property. Temperature-controlled, carefully ventilated and rigidly ordered and labelled, the state-of-the-art racks were packed with hundreds of bottles of wines, ports, liqueurs and spirits.

Milo moved through the shelves and selected two bottles of Burgundy. They would be perfect with dinner. Closing the cellar door behind him, he climbed the few steps up into the central area and glanced out of the full-length windows as he walked across the space. The blue of the Mediterranean shone in the early evening sunlight. He paused for a moment to take in the extensive view.

"For tonight," he said as he handed the bottles to his

chef. "Please make sure it has time to breathe properly."

Milo moved across the open-plan space to a large white sofa and resumed his seat. He glanced around the walls and smiled. A lot of time had been spent on the design of this particular area, hours thinking about how to dress the walls, floor and ceiling, and what lighting to use for each and every one of his precious exhibits. And tonight would see the culmination of five years of work amassing his collection.

"Everything has a value," he said as he gazed at a canvas entitled *The Seine at Argenteuil*. A Sisley and something he'd acquired from a private collector. He grinned as he thought about his grandfather. Value was something he had learnt from his ancestor. But the difference between Milo and the now-dead older man was that Milo knew that value came in many guises. To his grandfather, there was only one value, and that was always counted in money. To his grandfather, because money was king, anything could be afforded if you had enough of it, including favours and commodities as items for purchase. And the old gent never once flinched at murder, except when the price was not to his liking.

Now that Milo was in control of the family businesses, the blood that had tainted previous generations had been washed clean. Like the walls of the space where he now sat: sanitised, replanned, plastered, papered and painted. The extended room had been re-created so that as you moved from one area to another, the lighting and the ambience changed. For some areas music played in the background, and at the far end was a space for entertaining guests. Some evenings just for drinks and *canapés*, but tonight was for dinner. Milo's events were now more chic than those of his sometimes drug-fuelled youth. Dinner was always quieter, with fine cuisine, excellent wines and good conversation.

Milo breathed a contented sigh as his eye caught the corner of a large crate in one of the alcoves. At two-and-a-half metres by two metres, the container was too large to fit in the nook neatly and not be seen. Although that piece of untidiness was irksome, Milo's smile remained in place only because he wanted to savour the moment when he finally opened the package and revealed the precious cargo. It was an acquisition he had been seeking for quite some time. And now, here it was. In his special place, just waiting to be unpacked, examined, photographed, and then displayed where only he – and the few favoured guests he was expecting for dinner at eight – could see it.

messandrierre, sunday, june 2nd, 14.22

The afternoon sun was warm. The cold north wind of the previous few days had finally abated and been replaced by a more comfortable south-westerly breeze. The village was alive with people and families all enjoying the various displays of cars, vans, motorbikes and two vintage engines once used by the local *pompiers*.

"Your *papa* has done a wonderful job," said *Père* Chastain as he gazed at the gleaming motorbike.

"I helped as well," said Lucien, his chest puffing out like a strutting bird.

The old priest smiled. "I'm sure your contribution was invaluable," he said, ruffling Lucien's light-brown hair. "It must have taken…" The elderly man took a step back and gestured towards the bike. "I can only guess at the time, the effort and the emotion that is wrapped up in that." He tucked his hands behind his back and looked at Jacques.

"I wasn't keeping note," said Jacques. "But you're right. It took much more than just plain hard work." The remembered sound of his anger ricocheting around the garage walls as he beat out a crumple in the front mudguard was something he intended to keep to himself. Always. Along with the admission that the original had been hammered beyond redemption and had had to be replaced. He tightened his jaw.

The priest nodded. "If you ever want to talk, Jacques, you know where I am."

Père Chastain had made that offer on countless occasions since Beth's accident and subsequent death, and Jacques had never taken advantage of it. He preferred to keep things to himself. When he had needed to talk, it was always his sister Thérèse to whom he turned. She might be in Paris, and the distance could be considered a barrier, but during the dark times his phone calls to Thérèse had been a lifeline.

"Thanks," said Jacques. "Lucien and I are doing fine, but there may be something else you can help me with. I understand from Gaston that you know about art."

The priest's pale and wrinkled face creased into a beaming smile. "I once thought I would create beautiful pictures, but it was a childish fantasy. This is my real calling," he said, indicating the *soutane* he was wearing.

"Sorry, Father. I was led to believe that you had studied art or its history."

"Yes, I did. I've always been interested in the Renaissance period, which was my primary area of study, along with religious iconography. Ah, it was a long time ago, Jacques."

"I'm not sure that really matters. I just wanted to talk to you about a current case. I'm looking for some pointers as I don't know where to start." He reached into the back pocket of his jeans, pulled out the folded page containing the image of the painting and handed it over to the priest. "I was hoping you might recognise this."

Père Chastain glanced at the picture and then checked his watch. "I'm visiting Madame Pamier in a few moments. May I hold on to this, just for today?"

"Of course."

The priest nodded and looked at the page again before refolding it and putting it in his pocket. "I'm saying mass in Montbel this evening. I'll call at your chalet on my way back to Mende after that and let you know my thoughts."

"Thank you."

"Remind me, which chalet?"

"First on the left," chirruped Lucien.

The priest smiled. "*À plus tard*," he said as he turned and took his leave. Despite his age, there was the semblance of a spring in the old man's steps as he made his way across the crowded parking area and up the track towards *Ferme* Pamier.

Jacques scanned the milieu of people chatting and strolling between the vehicles before turning his attention to his son. Lucien was a world away. The sound of the bike's engine was a low hum in the back of the boy's throat as he leaned first one way and then the other. Jacques smiled. History was repeating itself, and Jacques cast his mind back to when he was a similar age, in Paris, sitting on his father's stationary motorbike, pretending he was driving it along the banks of the Seine, then out of the city and across mountains, fields and plains as he powered the vehicle along an imagined route.

Jacques' reverie was broken by a sudden screeching noise from Lucien, followed by an enthusiastic "Vroom! Vroom!"

"And I think that's enough for today," said Jacques.

Lucien frowned. "When can I have a bike like yours, *Papa*?"

"When you're as tall as the *Tour Eiffel*."

"That's what *Grand-père* always says." Lucien slipped down from the bike.

Jacques grimaced. Had he really said that? *So, I've finally become my father*. "And *Grand-père* is very wise," he said aloud. "He may be a bit forgetful at times, but you should still listen to what he says."

An announcement on the loudspeaker rang out across the gathering. The noise of the chatter barely subsided in response. Jacques checked his watch. It was almost time for the judging of the cattle.

"Shall we go and see the *Aubracs* and the other animals? Monsieur Fabien will be there." Jacques waited for Lucien to make a decision. Becoming a vet was Lucien's most recent wish for himself as an adult. Jacques wasn't sure how long that intention would remain, but he didn't want to deny his son any beneficial opportunity. Jacques watched as Lucien eyed the bike and then turned towards the field where the cattle would be paraded.

"But who will look after your motorbike?" he said as he turned back.

"It's all arranged," said Jacques, scanning the crowd. Pierre, the studious-looking only son of Marie and Martin

Mancelle, arrived just as the final call for the cattle-judging bellowed out over the crowd.

In amongst the stalls, under cover of a large marquee, Jacques kept to the fringe of a group of people drifting from one collection of produce to another, occasionally stopping in the aisle to chat and then moving on. In the background, the less-distinct announcements over the speaker system from the field continued. The goods of most of the traders held little interest for Jacques, but he did stop at the makeshift *fromagerie* and *boulangerie* to make some purchases. As he pocketed his change, he spotted a family with two young children standing by a much smaller table in the corner. The little girl was clutching a toy dog nestled in a small basket.

"I wonder…" Jacques whispered under his breath as he recalled Lucien asking about having a pet as a present for his next birthday. As the conversation played out in Jacques' head, he recalled the disagreement, followed by tears and a sulk that lasted until bedtime. *Maybe I was too harsh.* As the crowd in front of him moved forward, Jacques let his regrets fade away as all the solid and sensible reasons for not owning a dog flooded his mind. Who would look after it whilst he was at work? Wasn't Lucien too young to be responsible for a dog? After all, he couldn't even stack his shoes neatly or put his clothes away most of the time. Would having some responsibility, no matter how small, be good for Lucien? His brain was alive, buzzing again with all the possible reasons for and against becoming the owner of another living creature.

The family moved away, and Jacques watched as the little girl stroked and talked to her new toy dog. Her excitement and joy seemed to ripple through the crowd as she carefully cradled the plaything in her arms. Jacques decided to take a closer look. Striding around the people in front of him, he approached the vendor.

"Sorry, Monsieur, that was the last one." The seller stared Jacques in the eye. There was a defiance in his look, and in the tone of his voice, that made Jacques hesitate. The man maintained his stance: both hands balled and resting on the edge of the small but empty table. There was something odd about his accent, too.

"Will you be at the general market in Mende next Wednesday?"

The man shook his head and looked around to the entrance to the marquee.

"What about the *fête* at the end of this month?"

"Sorry, Monsieur." He began bundling the cloth on the table into a bag. Next, the small slatted, wooden table was collapsed and clasped under his arm. Before Jacques could ask another question, the man had pushed his way into the throng of people and disappeared.

As Jacques turned to leave, he noticed *Gendarme* Lefèvre and a representative from the *Mairie* gradually making their way through the tent on a tour of the stalls, checking licences and collecting payments on behalf of the municipality.

Jacques grinned. "Either that man was an unlicensed trader, too mean to pay, or an opportunist," he said to no one in particular. "That explains a lot." Pulling his phone out of his pocket, he quickly typed out some notes about the vendor: hair colour, stature, a description of the cloth, the table and the toy dog. He grinned to himself. *Beth was right.* "Always the policeman," he muttered to himself.

Looking across the crowd again, he saw the little girl and her parents standing at the entrance to the tent. Jacques hurried through the bustle of people. If luck was on his side, he might be able to get the trader's name from them if they knew it.

"Monsieur," He waved to try and attract the family's attention. They moved out into the sunshine. Jacques stepped left and right, trying to avoid people in his bid to follow them. As he emerged into the warm afternoon air and surveyed the field and the parking area beyond, the family and the seller were nowhere to be seen.

"Damn it!" He pocketed his phone and strode towards

the judging area. At one end of the field was a table with various cups, shields and rosettes, and Fabien, aided by Lucien, was handing out the prizes. The unlicensed trader could wait for another day, Jacques decided.

sunday, june 2nd, 19.32

"*Bonsoir, Père* Chastain." Lucien held open the little white gate for the priest to pass through.

"*Bonsoir, mon enfant.*" The priest carefully closed the gate.

"*Papa*'s on the porch," said Lucien as he jumped back on his bicycle and pedalled along the short drive.

"Isn't it time for you to be in bed? The priest smiled at his small escort before mounting the steps.

"Not quite yet," said Jacques, glancing at his watch. "There's still half an hour for you to play, or you can sit here with us."

Lucien shook his head and turned his bike around. In no time he was at the perimeter of the garden, cycling along the fence.

Jacques smiled at his visitor. "Please, sit down," he said, indicating the chair opposite.

The older man put the large heavy book he was carrying on the table and settled himself.

"The rise on this road gets steeper every day," he said, taking a deep breath and carefully folding back the front board and several pages of the book. He turned the volume to face Jacques. Removing the picture of the painting Jacques had given him earlier, he unfolded it and placed it beside the text.

"I'm not entirely sure, but this looks like a Vallade to me." The priest shoved his spectacles onto the top of his head and pointed to the figures on the beach in the foreground. "The use of perspective, the positioning of the people, and the colour palette, all suggest to me that this could be a Vallade."

"Is he especially famous or well known?"

"Oh yes. Very much so," said the priest. "What has been testing my mind all afternoon is that there is something familiar about the picture, but I just can't place it."

"So it could be valuable, then?"

"Most certainly. Of course, the actual value will depend on the provenance. Do you know its history at all?"

Jacques shook his head. "All I have is that image of the picture, plus a copy of a newspaper article from more than forty years ago about a court case pertaining to a legal challenge in respect of a bequest. I haven't looked into that yet. And this," he said, handing over the page of information printed from the internet.

Père Chastain put the page aside without even looking at the content. "A bequest? That could mean many things."

"Yes. I'll know more once I'm back in my office in Mende and can undertake the necessary research. The newspaper article gives little detail other than acknowledging that a preliminary hearing occurred in Paris at that time, and the expected outcome was an out-of-court settlement."

"I see." The priest returned his attention to the picture. "What makes me think it's a Vallade is the artist's use of the colour yellow. It's a particular shade, and it takes your eye through the painting. It was a sort of trademark of his." The older man pointed to the open page in the book he had brought. "This is one of his later paintings. This path stretches through the foreground right to the horizon and the hills in the distance," he said as he traced the route through the scene with a gnarled, arthritic forefinger. "The figure in the foreground on the right is touching his cap, and below the gate is a small clump of wild flowers with a few simple brushstrokes to indicate red petals. Now follow the colour."

Jacques looked at the picture of the whole canvas and found his attention hopping from one spot of red to the next until he reached the far distance, where the merest hint of pink on the lower edge of a cloud bounced his attention back to the figure at the gate.

"Clever. Very Clever."

"Now look at the picture you've been asked to find." *Père* Chastain placed the page that Jacques had given him on top of the book. "Once you understand the artist's mind, it's difficult to see his pictures in any other way."

Jacques looked at the scene. His eyes immediately spotted a tiny dash of bright yellow close to the bottom right of the painting, representing the child's sand-bucket. He followed the colour to the almost indiscernible splash of a yellow ribbon in the child's hair, then on to the detail on the woman's dress to the child's left, then further into the background and the cushion on which a man was lounging, then the parasol at the edge of the water and up to the faintest streak of pale gold in the bottom of a bank of clouds.

"Yes, I understand what you mean." Jacques lifted the piece of paper and held it at arm's length. Even at that distance, he couldn't make his eyes travel through the scene in any other way. "That's..." Jacques was lost for words. He dropped the page onto the table. "Where would I go to learn more about this particular painter?"

The priest grimaced. "I believe his paintings are mostly here in France, so the Louvre is a starting point. Probably the major galleries in Marseille and Lyon, too. As for a complete listing of his work, and therefore which of his paintings are in private ownership, in galleries or lost, I'm not sure. I only have one small section in this particular book, but I would expect, if you contact the Louvre, they will be able to answer that question for you."

The priest picked up the page with the beach scene on it, examined it again, and then turned to the text on the reverse. "I don't know if you've noticed this, but what it says here may be helpful, Jacques."

"But I don't think any of that text relates to the picture I need to find."

"You're right. It doesn't. But this snippet of information here may be useful." The old man pointed to the listing in the bottom left corner. "Listings like this are common in catalogues that galleries produce for specific exhibitions."

"So, the painting I'm looking for could have been on display somewhere…" Jacques looked at the notes and then at the text. "English," he said. "An exhibition somewhere in England, perhaps?"

"That's possible. But large galleries across the world print exhibition catalogues. Paintings of note often go from one gallery to another and can be absent from the originating gallery or private owner for several, sometimes many, years."

Jacques stared at the page from the catalogue. "So, that could be anywhere where English is spoken. America, Australia…" When he looked across the table he saw that the priest wasn't paying any attention. He was carefully reading through the page of notes from the internet.

Père Chastain eventually looked up and smiled. "There are two schools of thought on Impressionism," he said, handing the page back to Jacques. "For some, the Impressionist era lasted only a couple of decades. As it quite rightly says here, the movement began in Paris with a group of artists who were producing work in a particular style from the late 1860s up to the closing years of the 1880s. It was at that point the group of artists each went their own way. But some believe that Impressionism continued after that. Major artists – Monet, Renoir, and Pissarro – all continued painting into the twentieth century; Monet right up until 1926. So there are a lot of people who believe that Impressionism remained and finally died along with Monet. I don't agree with the notes on there. I'm not sure that I would class Vallade as an Impressionist. Of course, there are similarities in style, and I'm no expert, but Vallade… He's just not in the same class as Monet and the others, in my humble opinion."

Jacques grinned. "Thank you, Father. It would appear I have a lot of work to do."

The old man nodded and stood. "If I can help with anything else, Jacques, just ask." Hefting the book into his arms, he turned to leave.

"Perhaps you could leave me your book for a week or

so?"

"By all means." The priest replaced the tome on the table.

"Lucien, open the gate for *Père* Chastain, please, and then come in." Lucien sped across the lawn and was already standing at the entrance to the garden like a sentry before the elderly man had reached the end of the path.

"Sweet dreams, *mon fils*," said the priest as he left.

mende, monday, june 3rd, 09.36

The first day of the working week was often a late start for Jacques – especially following a holiday, no matter how short. Marshalling his son after any kind of break from the usual school routine was becoming more testing. There were times when Jacques was convinced that Lucien was deliberately trying his patience.

Finally breezing into his office in Mende, Jacques dumped his bag on his chair and went straight through to the room where his team worked.

Looking tanned and relaxed, Didier Duclos was at his desk sorting through the few bits of post that had arrived over the weekend. Maxim was engrossed in his regular morning scan of the online and printed newspapers. The studious quietude signified it was just another day.

"*Bonjour*," Jacques announced to the room as he entered. "Didier, good to have you back. How was your time away?" Jacques perched on the corner of a free desk.

"I'm glad to be back, but I think I have a lot to catch up on." Didier glanced at the various piles of paper in front of him.

"And the trip? How did that go?"

Didier smiled. "I didn't get as far as Corsica as intended, but…" He shrugged. "That didn't matter. I just hopped from one small port to the next, keeping close to the coast. The boys joined me at Fréjus, but my daughter-in-law wouldn't even get on the boat when it was moored at the marina. I spent a week there, and then Yves – you remember him, he helped us with the Gautier case – he met me a little further round the coast, and we spent a week in port at Théoule." Didier shook his head. "Yves is failing fast, Jacques. It was difficult, at times, to see him struggling as he walked along the marina." A deep frown on his face, Didier looked across the room. The pause seemed to be interminable.

Jacques broke the silence. "How far did you get in the end?"

"Not much further. My last mooring before turning back was at Port le Napoule."

"And the boat?"

Didier grimaced. "It's been a nice idea for as long as it has lasted, but the reality of sailing solo is more difficult than I imagined. It's a young man's game. Although I hadn't sailed since I was eighteen, I was surprised at how much I remembered and how much came back to me as my instinct kicked in. But for a man of my age…" He shrugged. "That type of adventure is past now." He shifted in his chair and began moving the bits of post around on his desk. "I'm thinking about a small river cruiser for my next trip." When Didier looked up, Jacques could see the light in his colleague's eyes and the glimmer of a smile on his face.

"When you've caught up, come through. We've got a new case, and I think it will mean a lot of work."

"OK, and Alain Vaux left a message saying he would drop in to see you this afternoon."

As Jacques walked back to his office, he wondered what Alain Vaux might want. He mentally ran through all his business commitments to his old boss and Chairman of the Board for the Vaux Group of businesses. Nothing was outstanding; he was sure of that.

Switching on the coffee machine and setting it going, he turned to look at the whiteboard. The meagre state of the business finances was starkly reflected in the three entries that barely covered the first third of the large board. Maxim had carefully updated each entry. The commission from the security company in the city had finally been paid for a home alarm system that Jacques had recommended three months earlier. The second case was another home security visit for Wednesday morning, and the final note on the board related to a forty-eight-hour house-sit three weeks previously. Jacques stared at the blank space on the right.

"Payment still outstanding," he muttered. He picked up a long magnetic strip and added it to the board below the last note. With the marker, he added the date, and an entry in the column headed *Nom* followed by a description in the next space.

"Madame *Point d'Interrogation*," he muttered as he added an abbreviated note, *Mme ?*, and then *C&T œuvre d'art*, to indicate that the case was a search and find for a work of art. Stepping back to his desk, he read and re-read the entries. The information didn't change, nor did it inspire. *What am I doing here?*

Jacques rested his bum against the edge of his desk; his long legs stretched out in front of him. The cases listed on the board were going to do very little to raise the profile of the business or bring in enough cash to make any form of dent in the losses already accrued.

"We're going to need to make some more efficiencies. But where?" He looked over his desk. His large desktop computer and those in the main office had all been returned to the Vaux Group to reduce costs for equipment rental and technology refresh. The laptops they each had now had been recently purchased from Vaux rather than accepting a planned upgrade. The result reduced ongoing costs, but meant that any future technology upgrade or replacements would have to come out of their own finances.

Jacques shook his head. "What other options… Unless…" It struck Jacques that perhaps Alain Vaux might be able to help. A re-negotiation of office space costs might be possible even if it was only for the short-term. Jacques nodded as he tried to persuade himself that it would work.

"I'll talk to Alain when he calls this afternoon." He moved around the desk and took his seat. The work still had to continue, no matter what. He opened his laptop and logged in just as his mobile rang.

"*Allo.*" Jacques listened. "Yes, both Lucien and I are well, thank you. How can I help you, Michelle?" Michelle, previously the Human Resources Manager at the Vaux Group, now had a seat on the board along with the lofty title of HR Director, and had become Alain Vaux's trusted deputy in his absence. She commanded a great deal of power within the organisation. As Michelle continued her side of the conversation, Jacques' smiling face gradually moved to a concerned deep frown.

"That's unfortunate," he said. "There was something in particular that I wanted to mention to Alain." He paused and listened. "Yes, either Didier or I will have a look at the documents as soon as they arrive," he said. "Yes… I'll get back to you as soon as I can."

"Damn it!" Jacques dumped his phone on the desk. As he looked up, Didier knocked on the open office door and walked in.

"Some post for you," he said, handing over a meagre five or six pieces of paper.

"Thanks. Alain won't be calling this afternoon after all. He now has an important meeting to go to that has been brought forward, and this afternoon was the only time that suited everyone."

"OK. But what about the work he wanted us to undertake?"

"Michelle is sending one of her team over with a file of papers in the next few minutes. She wants either you or me to look at them straight away."

"I'll handle that if you're busy with the new case, whatever it is." Didier looked over at the whiteboard. "Recovering art," he said as he turned back to face his colleague. "Are we sure we really want to take that on, Jacques?"

"I think we have to."

"Even though we have no contact details?" Didier glanced at the board again.

Jacques grimaced. "I know. She said she would be ringing me for daily updates, and I'm expecting a call today." He glanced at his phone. "But there's nothing so far. And she has asked that we exercise absolute discretion, Didier."

"So, there's no police involvement at all?"

Jacques shook his head and got up in response to the coffee machine's final gurgle. "A coffee?"

"No thanks. What, if anything, have we got on the artwork?"

"Just a copy of the painting on a page from some sort of catalogue for an exhibition," said Jacques as he returned to his desk, a full coffee cup in one hand and a saucer in the other. "My first task, I think, is to source that catalogue or book and to read up on the artist." He set the pieces of crockery down in separate places, pulled the large borrowed book from his bag, and carefully placed it between the cup and saucer.

Didier stared at the tome, his eyebrows shooting up to the top of his forehead. "I think I'll leave you to it," he said, and left.

***

In the main office, silence still reigned. As Didier resumed his seat, one of the security guards from the main entrance to the building came in and handed over the envelope he was carrying, with the slightest nod of the head. In a moment, he disappeared as swiftly as he had arrived.

Didier ripped open the large sealed envelope. Inside were various documents, all pinned behind a lengthy typed note from Michelle. Didier settled down to read the missive.

monday, june 3rd, 11.18

Jacques hurried down boulevard Henri Bourrillon and took a left into rue des Écoles. His destination, the Lamartine Library, was in place du Foirail. Standing outside the main entrance, he pulled out his wallet and searched for his library card. He was sure he still had one. But when he thought about it, he realised that it had been more than five years since he had last used the library. Giving up on finding any evidence that he was still a member, Jacques went in and stuffed his wallet back into his jacket pocket.

As always, the ambience of the building was hushed and slow, almost as if within those walls time ran at a silent half-speed. Jacques made his way to the Arts section and began scanning the shelves. He'd decided that if he could find the required books, he would deal with the missing library card or a new registration when he had to.

The bibliography at the back of *Père* Chastain's book on art, and the internet searches he'd carried out that morning, had shown that for the artist, Charles-Marcel Vallade, there were numerous books about his life and his work. In particular, Jacques wanted one of a series of books that formed a complete and definitive catalogue of his *œuvre*. On the lowest shelf, he found Vallade. Towards the end of the selection of books, he found the large foolscap volumes he wanted.

Getting down on one knee, he worked his way through the titles on the spines.

"'Volume Two, Portraiture in Oils, Three, Still Life in Oils, Four, Sketches, Drawings and Watercolours'." He re-checked the titles. The one he wanted, *Volume One, Landscapes in Oils*, appeared to be missing. He checked the shelf above, hoping the book might have been misfiled. As he stood up, he noticed a library assistant wheeling a small cart containing books.

"Madame, excuse me," he whispered to catch her attention.

The woman stopped. "Monsieur, how can I help?"

Her response was at a normal speaking level, and it took Jacques a couple of moments to register that and adjust his reply accordingly.

"I'm looking for Volume One of the Vallade Catalogue," he said. "It doesn't seem to be here."

The assistant quickly scanned the shelf, nodded and then went to one side of her cart. "I have it here," she said, holding up the book.

"Thank you." Jacques took the book from her, moved to one of the tables, and sat down. His original plan had been a quick flick through the book to find what he was looking for, a few moments to make any relevant notes, and then leave without the necessity of any possible library red tape. Opening the first few pages, he quickly realised that his search would not be so easily executed.

The book was organised chronologically. Jacques had no idea of the date when the painting he was looking for had been produced. Turning to the back, he found an extensive index and several appendices. But as he didn't have a title for the painting in question, nor the name, date or place of exhibition, the additional listings were of no use either.

He slapped the book shut. "This is going to be a page-by-page search," he sighed. "All two hundred and eighty of them." Getting up, he tucked the book under his arm and made his way to the desk and his next problem. Was he still a member or not?

monday, june 3rd, 14.28

Despite having had lunch and, therefore, almost a two-hour respite from the assistant at the library, Jacques' temper had not stilled. The form-filling had rankled even though he was clearly shown as being on the database. But the woman had insisted, even though Jacques had assured her none of his personal details had changed in the last five years. As he strode into his office, he slung his bag onto the sofa opposite the windows and marched to the coffee machine.

"A stiff drink would be more appropriate," he muttered, as he filled the machine with water and set it going. "And where did she get her attitude from?" He shook his head as he grabbed his bag and moved to the desk. "Next time, I'll send Maxim to fetch…" He slumped down in his chair as he realised he would do nothing of the sort.

"Work," he told himself as he pulled out the catalogue he'd borrowed from the library and set it on the desk. "I hope that woman's not there when I have to take this back."

He turned to the first page and grabbed a pen and some paper. *This is going to take some time.* He looked at the heading.

"Best to start at the beginning," he told himself.

INTRODUCTION

> *I've made all my paraphernalia portable. I can go anywhere, paint wherever I choose. I can respond to the light at a moment's notice. I can capture the light, the dark, the shadow, and every shade between as the colours change before my eyes... I must always be able to see the light.*
>
> —*Charles-Marcel Vallade, 1906*

The extensive and formidable reputation of Charles-Marcel Vallade as a landscape artist is undeniable. Through this catalogue I intend to explore this premise in detail. I will be examining his work from the very earliest sketches that are available, through his teenage years in Paris, and his later extensive body of work whilst living in Brittany and Normandy in later life, together with his work during his explorative travels as a young man across the whole of France and Italy.

I particularly want to investigate his use of colour and light – something that I have always considered to be rooted in the six months or so that he spent with Claude Monet at Giverny. Vallade was still a boy of sixteen at that time, and the influence of the older more renowned artist is clearly visible in Vallade's earliest works. I want to follow the development of those initial ideas for the use of colour and light, and I hope you will, by the time you reach the end of this treatise, come to see how much his attitudes, his capability, and his vision as an artist changed over time.

The paintings and panels contained and discussed in this volume will take you on a journey of exploration into the mind of an artist. You will come to understand his sureness of eye, his exactitude when recording the grandeur of wide vistas, or the smallest and most mundane moments of ordinary life. I also hope that you will develop an enduring love of his work and respect for his great talent.

Professor Gabriel Simmonet

monday, june 3rd, 20.38

In their apartment in Mende, Jacques looked at the envelopes from his post box that he'd dumped on the coffee table. They'd been sitting there since he and Lucien had first arrived home. It was one particular brown envelope that he was avoiding. No, not avoiding: refusing to acknowledge its presence. But as the brown one was larger than the others, it was becoming very difficult to ignore for much longer.

Jacques picked up the offending piece of post. It had come from England. He could feel the knot in his stomach that had first formed when he collected the post tightening even more. Pushing the envelope to one side, he glanced at the others: a couple of bills, probably, and what looked like a statement from a bank where some of his savings were invested. After a moment, he scooped up all of the mail and shoved it in his bag. It had been a long day. The woman at the library had been incredibly officious. When Lucien arrived at the office after school the boy was overtired and crabby, which rubbed off on Jacques, as much he had tried not to let that happen.

At bedtime Lucien could barely keep his eyes open, and Jacques had read little more than a couple of paragraphs of his son's current favourite story before he crept out of the boy's room.

In the quiet of the apartment, with the monitor on the table, Jacques could hear the steady and gentle breathing. He smiled. The challenging mud-coloured envelope could wait until tomorrow.

The evening was warm, and Jacques took the catalogue of Vallade's landscapes and moved out onto the balcony. With the copy of the picture he needed to find resting on the seat of the empty lounger beside him, Jacques sat down on his chair and swung his legs up onto the long cushion. The book resting against one raised knee, he turned to the introduction and began to re-read the opening paragraphs. It was essential to be sure he hadn't missed any possible nuance in the words because his mind had been so distracted earlier.

Jacques paused to properly consider the paragraphs he'd just read for the second time. He gave himself some moments to absorb the content. It was a relatively short introduction, but it was heartfelt. He sat back and gazed at the vista in front of him. The forest, the crags and outcrops of the mountains, and behind, the almost cloudless sky, the bright blue of the late afternoon having faded into a paler grey evening hue. *If Beth were here, she would know...* He looked away, consciously stopping his mind from pursuing the thought to its natural conclusion. He would have to work it out for himself.

"I think this piece of work is going to be long, slow, and tedious," he sighed. He sat forward, turned back to the first page and stared at the opening quote.

"A quote. From a paper he's written, perhaps." *Do artists write papers?* Jacques picked up his pocketbook as another thought came into his mind. *I suppose there could be diaries or letters to family or friends, maybe.* He jotted down a couple of notes.

"Professor Gabriel Simmonet... Might he still be alive?" He turned back to the page opposite the list of contents and carefully worked through the text. "Published 1998." Jacques jotted a note for himself to undertake an internet search for Simmonet.

Settling back with the catalogue on his knee, he continued to read the following section, making notes until almost midnight.

THE EARLY YEARS: 1888-1902

As a child, I never really understood the extent of her influence... time spent sketching together in the orchard or on the cliffs, I now see was precious.... I never tired of looking at the sea or the coast. I still haven't. I never will.

—Charles-Marcel Vallade, 1928

Born in 1888 on the 17th of April, Charles-Marcel Vallade was the fourth child of Louis-Charles Vallade, a cider farmer, and his first wife Claudette, who died following the birth of twins when Charles-Marcel was just over two years old. With six mouths to feed and a young son and two baby girls to care for, Louis-Charles Vallade wasted no time in securing a new mother for his children. When the twins were barely eleven months old, Louis-Charles married Marie Sophie Bossuot, a school teacher from Quimper. It would be Marie Vallade who would become Charles-Marcel's primary guiding influence and later, one of his greatest critics.

Living in the Aulne valley in the département of Finistère, Charles-Marcel grew up amongst orchards, rolling countryside, rugged cliffs along the nearby coast, and a mostly temperate climate.

Charles-Marcel's father was a successful farmer and businessman, having inherited the thriving cider farm from his own father. The Vallade family had produced the now highly-prized and traditionally-brewed Cornouaille Cider for more than five generations by the time Charles-Marcel was born. The farmhouse still exists, but is no longer held by the family.

As a young child, Charles-Marcel and his two younger sisters were initially educated by their stepmother. At the age of four, Charles-Marcel lost his twin sisters when a bout of diphtheria swept through the community. He also suffered a lengthy illness as a result. Once recovered, the boy and his stepmother became inseparable.

Much later in life, in letters to friends, Charles-Marcel acknowledged the significant influence that his stepmother Marie Sophie Vallade had had in his life, his work and his style of painting.

tuesday, june 4th, 08.37

At the morning team briefing, Jacques turned to look at the whiteboard, grimacing as he once again noted the sparsity of the work. In the spare space, Jacques used a couple of magnets to secure the image of the painting to the board.

"This is what we need to find," he said, tapping it with the first joint of his forefinger. "And, no, I don't know the title yet. But I am gradually working my way through this." He held up the first volume of the catalogue.

"What details do we have, Jacques?"

"Not much, Didier. I know the artist, Charles-Marcel Vallade, was born in Finistère in 1888. His body of work is extensive, and the complete catalogue is in four volumes, all of around two hundred or more pages each. We will be searching for a single painting from about one to two thousand items of art."

Maxim let out a low whistle.

"And there's no guarantee that the catalogue holds every single item," Jacques continued. "I was talking to the local priest at the weekend. He studied art at one point, and it is possible that some of the items may have been destroyed or are just lost. Works in private ownership are listed in the catalogue, but again there's no guarantee that all of them are there."

"What about the dark web, Jacques? Art is sometimes traded and used as revenue in exchange for drugs or arms."

"That's right," said Maxim. "I can take a look and see what I can find. There are some dark forums out there, too. I can ask some questions."

"Yes, Maxim, please do that, but be discreet. And make sure you check bona fide sites too. I don't want this picture to come up for sale at a genuine auction house, and we miss it because we concentrated our efforts in the wrong place."

"But if it's been stolen," said Maxim. "Then that's not likely—"

"We don't know if it has been stolen. Yet." Jacques cut him off a little more sharply than intended. *I should have called it a night earlier than I did.* "Sorry Maxim. The owner is insisting that the painting is just missing."

Didier frowned. "So, it could be out on loan? If that's the right term. Is that what you mean, Jacques?"

"I think it's possible. I'm also becoming very suspicious of Madame ? and her intentions. She said she wanted daily updates and that she would call me yesterday. There has been no contact from her since we met last week. I can't call her because she hasn't given me contact details, and, as you know, Maxim, the only numbers she has used previously were unobtainable. And now I have a question about why someone would need three possible burner phones to instigate a genuine commission for work to be done. That question is constantly going around in my head, but I can find no answer. Is she really as anxious about the artwork's return as she appeared when I met her?" He shrugged.

Didier nodded. "Is she trying to pull a fast one over the genuine owner, perhaps?"

"I don't know. But Madame ? says she legally owns the painting. And there is another piece of research to undertake. Maxim, can you find out where this newspaper cutting came from?" Jacques handed his colleague the piece of newsprint he had received.

Maxim stared at the small rectangle of fragile paper. "I'll see what I can do, but it won't be easy, Jacques."

"Take whatever time you need. We've no limits on this commission, and I'm not going to impose any. I hope Madame ? has the funds to pay for the work if this drags on for months and months. I also want you to check for any wills, legal documents, court papers concerning Charles-Marcel Vallade. I expect they will all be in Paris." Jacques consulted his notebook. "He died in August 1972."

"OK," said Maxim, a broad grin spreading across his

face. "This is just how it used to be."

Jacques smiled. *Let's hope it stays this way for the foreseeable future.* Keeping the thought to himself, he turned to Didier.

"There's one other thing that we need to do," he said, as he handed over a photocopy of the information from the reverse of the page containing the image of the painting. "*Père* Chastain tells me that the information on there, about a completely separate work of art entitled 'Child in the Park', is useful, because that painting and the one we are interested in finding must, at some point, have been exhibited together. So, if we can identify the artist for 'Child in the Park' and trace the exhibition, we should—"

"Be able to find our painting in the catalogue for the same exhibition," interrupted Didier.

"Yes," said Jacques. "Can you take that piece of research forward, please, Didier?"

"Of course."

"If and when you trace the details of the exhibition, get in touch with the relevant gallery or galleries and find out who gifted or loaned the artwork we are seeking. It will help us build a detailed provenance."

Didier grinned. "Galleries, provenance. You're starting to sound like an antiques dealer, Jacques."

Maxim chuckled quietly, and Jacques just rolled his eyes. "Perhaps. I just think we need to be thorough, as we always are. It might be worth checking any associated terms and conditions surrounding the 'gift' or 'loan'." Jacques underlined the two words with a toned emphasis.

"OK," said Didier as he quickly jotted some notes. "But what about the security visit due tomorrow morning? I'd assumed you'd want me to do that."

Jacques nodded. "Yes, please, Didier. But I'd like us to pick up the research for the second painting as soon as possible. If you could fit that around the security visit, that would be helpful. I will be following up on a possible line of enquiry with the author of the art book: Professor Gabriel Simmonet. I want to see if he is available to talk about

Vallade, and I want to know his sources for the information in the book. Some of it is extremely detailed, and he uses quotes from Vallade himself, but he doesn't always attribute them. I think there may be an archive somewhere holding a significant body of papers."

Didier nodded. "Don't those books have a list at the back with details of the sources used or documents consulted?"

"Unfortunately, not this one. But I've only got the first volume. There are three others, and I suppose the type of list you're referring to may be at the back of the last book." *Another trip to the library. I just hope that woman isn't there.*

Jacques glanced at the whiteboard. "The last thing is the outstanding invoice. Maxim, can you follow that up, please?"

"I've already contacted the house owners twice, Jacques, and payment has been promised within the week each time, but nothing has come through."

"And it is the owner, Monsieur Bernot, that you have spoken to, isn't it?"

"Err, no." Maxim started chewing the end of his biro. "It's just that…" He put the pen in his shirt pocket and cleared his throat. "The person I've been talking to is someone who works for the family, and I know her from when we were at the *lycée* together. She was a toxic piece of work back then, and I don't think she's changed. Since she found out I work here, she's been ringing and messaging me constantly. I've blocked her email address twice, but she gets around that by creating a new one. It's just awkward and annoying."

"Alright," said Jacques. "We'll handle this a little differently. Can you draft a letter or an email addressed directly to Monsieur Bernot stating that we've issued the invoice, but payment still has not been received. Add that any further delay will mean that we will impose a twenty per cent surcharge if they don't settle within the next seven days. You might also want to include that any further tardiness will incur a secondary level of a compound daily surcharge at five per cent per day."

Maxim's eyes widened. "Can we really do that?"

"Yes and no," said Jacques. "Our terms and conditions stipulate that a penalty may be imposed if payment for work is not received on time. But we don't specify what that penalty might be."

Maxim frowned. "OK. So, do I let you see the draft before I send it, Jacques?"

Didier jumped in before Jacques could respond. "I'll look at the draft for you, Maxim."

"OK, Thanks. And if they ring to argue about the extra charges?"

"I doubt that they will," said Jacques. "Can we make sure that the letter or email goes out today, please?" He looked from one colleague to the other, and they both nodded.

Maxim smiled. "Thanks." He stood. "Do you need me for anything else?"

Jacques shook his head and returned to his desk. "The papers that Michelle sent over, Didier. What was that all about?"

Didier waited until the door had clicked shut behind their younger colleague. "At the moment, it's just a full background check on a client of Alain's that is being difficult."

"Difficult? In what way?"

"He's a property developer who has shown great interest in a parcel of land in the Vaux Group's portfolio. It was an old olive grove on the outskirts of Marseille that Vaux purchased at the end of last year. Alain has obtained appropriate permissions for planning and building purposes and has prepared the site for services, gas, water, electricity to be installed. So Vaux has made a significant investment since acquiring the tract. This particular client registered an interest in the plot within a couple of days of it being put on the market for sale. But some of the client's proofs aren't up to scrutiny, and Alain is concerned."

"Much progress so far?"

"Not yet, but I understand Alain's concerns. Some of the

statements proffered as surety are for closed bank accounts."

"That's an odd way to do business."

Didier nodded. "I'm checking for evidence of current and viable assets."

"Let me know if you need any help with that. Just keep digging."

Didier moved across the room and turned back. "Jacques, you do know we have a small art gallery here in Mende, don't you?"

"No, I didn't."

"It's immediately behind the basilica on rue du Soubeyran. It might be worth a look."

"Thanks, Didier. I can call in on my way to collect Lucien from school later in the week."

Finally, alone in his office, Jacques pulled the catalogue of Vallade's work out of his bag and placed it on the desk. As he did so, the post he'd shoved in the night before slipped out onto the floor. Jacques looked down, and on the top of the scattered envelopes was the one from England. A knot began to arrange itself in his stomach again. It could only mean one thing. The hoops he'd been made to jump through, all the accommodations he'd accepted over the past year for his mother-in-law, had not been enough. He shook his head when he mentally counted the appeasements he'd agreed to. He could feel the warmth of his blood rising through his neck as he thought of the inordinate amount of time he'd expended on the woman's demands – often at the expense of his own business.

"I know the amount of security and investigative work we have is low at the moment," he said as he reached down and scraped the envelopes off the floor. "But you haven't helped, Madame." He tapped the long edge of the brown envelope against the desk. The interval between the taps became shorter as his breathing quickened.

"Damn it!" He ripped the short edge of the envelope clean off. The destruction of the covering and its contents mirrored his deepest fear. Separating the white pieces of paper from the brown, he set them out flat on the catalogue and lined them up so that he could read the entire document. He got little further than the first three paragraphs. His hands clenched into fists, crumpling the pages, and he hurled the ball of paper across the room. Grabbing his mobile, he scrolled through his contacts and dialled.

"Bruno, I need your help. Can we meet? ... OK. I'll be there in twenty minutes."

tuesday, june 4th, 09.41

Investigating Magistrate Bruno Pelletier, now happily retired, read Jacques' entire letter in complete silence. Having reached the end, he removed his spectacles and began to clean them on his handkerchief.

Jacques grinned. It was the closest he'd come to a smile since the letter had arrived the day before. But Bruno's all-too-familiar habit of toying with his glasses was somehow usual and comforting at that moment.

"Let's sit down, shall we?" Bruno pulled out two old three-legged stools from under the bench in his substantial greenhouse. "This is a tough and delicate situation, and there's only one *avocat* that I would recommend."

"Who?" Jacques swiped the back of his hand across his forehead. The heat in the greenhouse was causing beads of sweat to bud on his brow.

"Audrey Taillard. I'll give you her contact details before you leave. But what about Lucien? Does he know anything about this?"

Jacques perched on the edge of the stool. "Nothing. I've told him nothing, and I intend to keep it that way."

"Where is this stance of your mother-in-law's coming from, Jacques?" Bruno put the pages of the letter down on the workbench and crossed his arms. "Does she genuinely believe that she is the better parent for your son?"

"I'm sure she does think that. But why she can't accept all the accommodations we've already agreed on, I just don't know. She has access to her grandson. I've made sure of that. But a residency order..." Jacques ran his hand through his hair. "I just don't understand what she hopes to achieve other than to pay a lot of money to a bunch of lawyers."

"How old is Lucien now?"

"He'll be seven in August, but at times, some of the things he says, you'd think he was forty-seven!"

Bruno smiled. "It's going to be difficult to keep this from him, Jacques."

"Perhaps. But I don't want Lucien to get upset or to feel insecure in any way, and I'd rather he knew nothing until it, well, if it becomes necessary to tell him."

"Custody battles can be very damaging, Jacques."

Jacques pulled at the back of his shirt as a thin trickle of sweat seeped down his spine. "I know. But I think it's important to protect him from this as much as possible."

Bruno nodded. "Ah. And if the *avocat*, in order to seek a resolution that means residency remains with you, suggests increasing access for your mother-in-law, what will you do then?"

Jacques let out a long sigh. *More time spent in the UK. The business will probably have to go.* He stared at the row of carefully-potted orchids on one side of the hothouse. *What else can I do? Returning to the police force is no answer because of the hours. What other occupation can I take up that would ensure I can handle the cases I'm used to working on, while facilitating being the only parent of a young child with a family on the wrong side of the Channel?*

"I don't know," he said eventually. "I just don't know. But she will NOT take my son."

Bruno folded the papers and handed them back. "Get in touch with Audrey and let her guide you through this. She's the best person for the job. Come, I'll get you her number."

Bruno got up, and Jacques felt a light touch on his shoulder as his old friend moved past him and walked towards the house.

tuesday, june 4th, 10.49

Back in his office, Jacques added Audrey Taillard's details to his list of contacts and typed a note into his calendar for the weekend. The *avocat* was currently in Paris, and any discussions about his mother-in-law's application for a residency order would have to be undertaken over the internet. Lucien had a friend's birthday party coming up. It would be the perfect time to talk to the lawyer.

Jacques slumped down in his chair, the catalogue of Vallade's work still open on the desk where he had left it.

"I don't even want to think about that," he complained as he shoved the book to one side. *I need to focus.* Taking a deep breath, he closed his eyes for a minute or two and remained absolutely still. *Madame Williams won't win.*

"I can't let her win," he said, opening his eyes again. Standing, he moved across to the windows and leaned against the glass. His gaze darted around the office, momentarily focussing on the walls, the floor, the whiteboard, and finally coming to rest on Lucien's little corner of office space. Jacques pinched the bridge of his nose. "And getting emotional won't help."

Finally deciding that a strong cup of coffee might temper his still-out-of-control thoughts, he crossed to the machine and flicked the switch. Returning to his desk, he picked up the catalogue and the eight foolscap pages covered on both sides with his notes. There was still so much more information to take in.

"There's a painting to identify and locate," he said. The coffee machine was still working as Jacques carried the papers and the catalogue from his desk and moved across to the settee opposite the windows. The change of view will help, he thought. Waiting for the coffee to brew, he flicked through the remaining pages and sighed as he realised he was barely a third of the way into the book. He turned back to the paragraphs he had most recently read, alongside copies of the works by Vallade. The detailed explanations mused on the composition, the use of colour, and the brushwork.

He made himself comfortable, resigned to another few hours of reading and note-taking.

STUDENT YEARS IN PARIS: 1902-1904

The money's all gone. I'm tired, hungry, with nowhere of my own to stay, but I'm alive. I'm learning so much... The city is very noisy. So many people. I want to capture some of the buildings and the architecture. Not the great and noble buildings such as the Opera House. The small buildings. The detail of a flowered balcony outside an apartment. The doorway of a bargee's house, a woman feeding the pigeons on her doorstep, or a small courtyard when the washing line is out... The details of ordinary lives.

—*Charles-Marcel Vallade, 1903*

At the age of fourteen and encouraged by his stepmother, Vallade left home to go to Paris. More romantic writers than myself paint a picture of the artist as a young man who felt the need to escape his controlling and overbearing father. But letters written home, and later articles in news journals, indicate that this is not the truth. Vallade's stepmother actively persuaded him to leave. She gave him some money that she had saved and she put him in touch with a distant relative who lived near Montmartre.

Madame Vallade's distant relative was the great-niece of Berthe Morisot, a renowned impressionist painter who began as a copyist for the Louvre art gallery in the centre of Paris. Charles-Marcel also began his career as a copyist by accompanying his kinswoman to the gallery.

Although related, the family did not honour that status. Vallade was housed in the servants' quarters and was used as a groom, and occasionally as a kitchen hand fetching coal and wood for the ovens. Writing to his stepmother he complained about '*the roughness*' of his '*hands*' because he undertook '*the work of a skivvy.*' In a later letter, possibly in response to one from his stepmother indicating her concerns for her adopted son, he said...

'*...the work may be demeaning and demanding, Maman, but it makes the time spent with my cousin in the Louvre that much more absorbing, uplifting and worthwhile. I am learning, Maman. You can not believe how much I am <u>learning</u>...*'

The underlining was Vallade's own. In my view it gives a very early indication of my contention that the artist was beginning to develop his eye for detail and colour. I doubt he recognised that at the time. It would be Monet who would make that clear to him later.

After almost a year with his relatives, Vallade decided to try and make his own way. In a letter to his stepmother in the early months of 1903, he informed her that he was living hand-to-mouth, existing on what few *sous* he could earn from selling his sketches on the streets of Paris.

One of his earliest known and recorded pieces of work is **S1** ***Flowers on a Balcony, Montmartre*** (Charles-Marcel Vallade Volume Four: Sketches, Drawings & Watercolours) dating from some time in 1903. The sketch was purchased by a businessman and art collector named Edgard Sol. Monsieur Sol went on to become Vallade's sponsor at the Academy of Art, and it was through Sol that Vallade was able to spend time with Monet. It was also Sol who later commissioned the oil version of the aforementioned sketch which is pictured overleaf.

tuesday, june 4 th, 14.08

Jacques was sifting through his copious pages of notes, crossing out some words and sentences and underlining others. On a couple of pages, whole paragraphs had been deleted as he'd gradually assessed each scrap of information in relation to the three criteria he had set himself: relevance to the investigation, relevance to the artwork in question, and key facts, data or evidence about Vallade in person.

As he got to the last page, he came across his note about Professor Gabriel Simmonet. *Might he have critical information about the painting and Vallade himself?* The answer that shot through Jacques' conscious mind was a resounding *Yes*. Abandoning his task of preparing all the notes to upload onto an information sheet on the shared drive, he turned to his laptop and did an internet-wide search.

The name Gabriel Simmonet brought up numerous references, one of the first being a page on Wikipedia. Jacques clicked the link and immediately checked the personal facts box on the right below a photograph of the professor. *Good-looking man. Intelligence shines out of that face.*

Born	Gabriel Laurent Simmonet
	18th June, 1921
	Lyon, France
Died	8th November, 2001, (aged 80)
	Paris, France
Nationality	French
Education	Lyon, Beaux-Arts Paris, London, New York

Known for	Art Historian, Author, and TV Presenter
Notable work	*Charles-Marcel Vallade : A Complete Catalogue of Works in 4 Volumes* *Impressionism World-wide*
Spouse	Annette (m. – 1996)
Children	Rose-Marie, Paul, André

As Jacques scanned the information, he noticed the only highlighted entries were the Central School of Fine Arts and Art History in Paris.

"No other pages about individual members of his family, and no date of marriage either."

Jacques read the first few paragraphs of text and decided to print the whole article. He clicked back to the search results. As he glanced down the page, it occurred to him that a search on some significant event in Simmonet's life or his eminent work might provide better results. The one event likely to have earned the professor a lot of newspaper coverage at the time was his death. Jacques typed in the professor's full name and the year of his death. At the top of the list of results was a lengthy obituary. Jacques settled back to read the digitised copy from a national broadsheet.

Following the initial facts and a couple of paragraphs about Simmonet's early life in Lyon, there was information detailing his time in New York and London and his post in Paris. His academic achievements were the subject of the next section of the article. It was the last sector that was the most interesting to Jacques. Simmonet and Vallade had first met in Paris in 1953. They had met again in Marseille the following year and again in 1955, when Simmonet had announced his intention to catalogue the full body of Vallade's œuvre. According to the article, thence had begun a regular correspondence that lasted until Vallade died in 1972. Jacques paused for a moment. *If the catalogue was not published until 1998, then who did Simmonet consult about the artwork?*

Jacques grinned. "There must be more letters. Somewhere," he muttered, as he decided to print off the article. He continued his search for more news coverage of Simmonet's death. The fifth item listed was another digitised article from an art magazine. This included a picture of Simmonet's parents' house in Lyon, a couple of other relevant photographs, and at the end a shot of the writer's family standing at the graveside. Underneath were the full names of each of his three children. Rose-Marie was listed as Madame Marie Rouvière.

"If anyone knows about Professor Simmonet as a father, it will be you, Madame." Jacques sent another document to the printer.

A quick look through the remaining items on the first page of results brought nothing of any particular note. Jacques scanned the second page and decided he had already identified the most salient elements. Getting up, he went through to the main office to collect his printouts.

"Maxim," said Jacques, as he picked up his prints and sifted out the sheet containing the image of the Simmonet offspring at their father's grave, "I have a photograph here, and I was wondering if you could do a reverse lookup for me, please?"

"Sure, who is it?"

Jacques put the page on his colleague's desk. "This woman here. That's Marie Rouvière, maiden name Simmonet, father Professor Gabriel L Simmonet. The picture is from 2001, so it is a bit grainy, but I was hoping you might be able to find out who she is, where she currently lives, and if she has a social media profile, what we might glean from the content."

Maxim looked at the copy and then at the source code on the bottom of the printed page.

"I'll go to the actual website, Jacques, and use that as a link for the lookup. That printed image is not good quality. Do you want me to get her birth, marriage and death details too?"

"Yes, please, but I'm hoping she's still alive as I want to

speak to her."

"Might have something for you by the end of the day, but the life events will take a little longer."

"Thanks, Maxim." Jacques gathered his other bits of paper together and turned to leave. "Come through as soon as you find anything," he said from the doorway.

Back in his office, Jacques settled down with a marker pen and began to note the pages for the critical facts or pieces of evidence to add to his handwritten notes.

Hearing a light tap on the office door, Jacques looked up from his research.

"Alain, come in." He stood and held out his hand for his visitor to shake. "Good to see you. It's been quite a while."

"It has, Jacques," said Alain Vaux as he took Jacques' hand and shook it firmly.

"Please sit," said Jacques indicating the chair opposite. "Coffee?"

"No thanks. I wanted to apologise in person for not being available to meet you yesterday afternoon as planned, but I was detained in Marseille."

"Don't worry about it. I know how it is."

Alain smiled. "I'm sure you do. However, there are two things that I want to discuss with you."

As businesslike as ever. "Of course," said Jacques keeping his thoughts to himself.

"You should have received some papers from Michelle about a possible client, and I want you to undertake a forensic background check on this man."

"This is," Jacques glanced at the whiteboard, "Milo Sforza," he said, quickly reading the notes that Didier had added late yesterday.

"I've met him already, Jacques, but there's something about him that has unnerved me." Alain sat with his legs crossed and his hands tightly clasped in his lap.

When it comes to business, nothing gets under your skin. Jacques frowned. "In what way?"

"That's part of the problem. I can't pinpoint what it is about the man that makes me very wary of him. Hmm," he said with a wry smile on his face. "If I were my father, I'd explain it all away by telling you I don't like the shine on his shoes."

Jacques smiled. "Interesting," he said. "But I need a bit more than that."

"And as silly as it seems, when I was first introduced to Monsieur Sforza last week, I found myself looking at his shoes, then his clothes, and his slicked-back, black hair." Alain paused and looked at the floor. "If I could explain it in sensible words, I would. But all I can say is that his shoes are too shiny. Too black. Everything about that man is just a bit too much. Perhaps, too 'right' – which makes me feel everything about him is false underneath."

"Alright," said Jacques. *This unsettling feeling is pure instinct.* He'd come across this before as a rookie policeman in Paris. *No, it was before that. The first time was at school.* He felt a lump in his throat, and consciously stripped the thought from his mind.

"I know what you're talking about, Alain," he said quickly. "There isn't a man on the force I've worked with who hasn't experienced that sort of sensation at some point in his career. Either out on the streets in uniform or working in plain clothes as a detective. It's your base instinct at work. And in my experience, it's always best to listen to it and to be cautious."

Alain smiled. "Thanks, Jacques. I was beginning to think I might have lost my edge. I've always prided myself on being able to read anyone sitting at the other side of a boardroom table. But Sforza… There's something about him that…" Alain frowned and shook his head.

Jacques nodded. "Didier is taking the background check forward, and as we only got the papers yesterday, it's a little too early for me to give you an update."

"No, Jacques," said Alain raising his hand to add emphasis. "That is not why I'm here. An update was the last thing on my mind. I needed to ensure that you fully understood my concerns about this man."

Jacques smiled. "If there's anything to find, Didier will

find it."

"Thanks." Alain got up, walked across to the windows, and stood there momentarily. Jacques watched as the tension his former boss had brought into the room gradually slipped from his shoulders.

"I always liked this view," he said, watching the street below.

Jacques often spent his thinking time standing in the same spot.

Alain turned and leaned against the glass. "I also wanted to see you today because I have a proposition for you."

"A good one, I hope."

"I think so." Alain straightened up to his full height and marched back to the chair. "The large open-plan office on the other side of this building will become free at the end of this month."

"The space occupied by the IT company?"

"Yes. When the tech company arrived, they were a small team of twelve and needed room to grow. They're recruiting again, and they've decided to look for other premises. They gave formal notice to quit on April 1st, and since then we've been negotiating get-out of the current contract and the offer of a new one for space in our building across the road."

And I bet I know which way that went. Jacques smiled.

"My proposition is to suggest that you take on the extra space if you like."

Jacques tried to contain his surprise and scratched his eyebrow. "I wasn't expecting that, Alain," he said after a pause, mentally calculating the extra costs the new space would attract.

"There are some strings attached," he said. "Should I go on?"

There are always conditions with you, Alain. "I'm listening."

"This idea has come from Michelle, and it's something that she has been lobbying for since last year. We, as an organisation, don't offer our staff any on-site childcare facilities. We expect them to use family or to pay for regular care whilst both parents are at work. Michelle has also undertaken some analysis, which is quite compelling considering our growing number of employees with young children. Michelle has successfully made the case that an on-site childcare facility would reduce time lost when parents are called away. There is likely to be an improvement in productivity if parents know that they can take five or ten minutes to cross the road to see their children during the day."

"And where would we fit into this plan, Alain?"

"Young Lucien, and Maxim's children, would be able to move out of your main room and use the new space. How is Lucien, by the way?"

"He's fine, thank you." Jacques refrained from mentally admonishing his old boss for not posing that question as soon as he had arrived. But that was Alain.

"Good," said Alain. "We were also wondering if Amélie would like to continue her role in your *crêche* as a member of the employed care team in the new space. Might she be interested in taking the manager's post?"

Jacques stared at his visitor. "That's a..." Jacques pushed his chair back from his desk. "That's a generous offer, Alain. I can't speak for Amélie, but I will talk to her. I will also talk to Lucien. As you can see, he has his own little office space over there, and he may not want to give that up."

"Nor should he," said Alain, with a broad smile. "Of course, if you are all agreeable, the set-up costs will be borne by Vaux, and we will refurbish your main office as part of the refit. Whatever Amélie decides, I will accept, but please let her know that whichever role she chooses, she will be paid at the standard rate plus two per cent for however much time she spends at the new facility."

A question crossed Jacques' mind, and he wondered if he should ask it now or after he'd spoken to Amélie.

"Alain, if you need staff for this new venture, shouldn't there be a specific recruitment exercise to obtain the best people for the job with the right qualifications? Amélie started our childcare space for just our own children; her only qualification was as a mother. Since then, we have paid for her to obtain the minimum level of certification."

Alain grinned. "Of course we want appropriately qualified staff, Jacques. But that doesn't stop us from initially appointing or recruiting internally. Recruiting externally is a significant set-up expense if the experiment subsequently fails to deliver the anticipated income. And even though you are now an independent organisation, I still consider you and your team as a… How shall I put it? A distant part of the Vaux family."

Jacques nodded. *Not quite a free choice, then.* "I will talk to Amélie and see what her views are. Will we be able to see the space? If she is interested, she might want to have a look."

"By all means. The present occupiers said they would be out by the end of this week. One day next week would be fine. Just check with Michelle's team before going in. They may have set up site visits and may have contractors coming in to quote for the refit."

He moved towards the door. "Anything you can get me on Sforza will be appreciated, Jacques." He hesitated at the threshold. "There's something else about that man. I've just realised that, although his French is excellent, there's a faint background accent, but I'm not sure of the origin." He nodded as if to confirm that his thoughts and words were accurate. "And I fully expect to see an invoice for the work, too."

"Alain, happy to work freely for you."

"No, Jacques, this is business. I expect to pay for Didier's time and expertise."

"Preferential rates, then."

Alain grinned. "If you insist."

Jacques smiled as the Chairman of the Board of the Vaux Group left his office.

Glancing across to his laptop from the notes and the papers he had been working through, Jacques realised that the impetus to get the information brigaded and uploaded onto the shared drive had deserted him. Instead, he picked up the catalogue for Vallade's work, moved across to the sofa and settled down. *More paintings and more stuff I don't fully understand.* He let out a sigh. *This is the strangest investigation I've ever had to handle.*

IMPRESSIONIST INFLUENCES: 1905-1906

I'm to go to Giverny Maman. Monsieur Sol is sponsoring me again, and I'm to meet the great artist Monet. I'm there to observe, to paint, to learn – nothing more. There will be no formal teaching, but can you imagine being able to watch such a great man at work.
—*Charles-Marcel Vallade, 1905*

Vallade arrived at Giverny in the autumn of 1905 and stayed for about six months. There are very few surviving letters from him for this period of his life. This has been explained in different ways over the decades, but I prefer to accept Vallade's own words when he was interviewed for an art magazine in 1932:

'...*I was spending as many hours as Monet himself in front of my canvasses. I followed his lead. I had no time for anything else. My mind was completely absorbed by colour and light...*'

In this section I want to explore Vallade's use of colour and light, and as we move through his body of work from this time I believe it becomes quite clear that his brush work changes and develops and his eye for detail, light, dark and shade is sharpened under Monet's influence.

His early work at Giverny reflects the season with an abundant use of russet, ochre, yellow and brown. **L22** *A Garden West of Paris*, completed some time in October or November 1905, is somewhat naïve in its execution, but the vibrancy of the colour palette is undeniable. Compare this directly with **L106** *Fields in Spring*, which was completed on April 4th, 1906, and you will see the change in the brush work, the greater attention to detail and refined use of colour. I believe this painting is the first in which Vallade uses his trademark principle of leading the viewers' eye through the picture along a particular and specified route. Look closely at the three, almost insignificant splashes of pale yellow on the corsage of the woman in the foreground, which is then echoed in the plants in the centre of the flowerbed in the middleground, and again on the hat of the man in the background.

← L22 *A Garden West of Paris*

tuesday, june 4th, 15.39

Jacques turned yet another page that did not take his search forward. But he had learned much more about the artist, and was beginning to understand what must have been Vallade's primary objectives as a painter. About to start the next section of the book, he looked to his right. The coffee was there, still waiting to be poured. He decided to give it a miss.

"Jacques, I've made some headway on the second picture," said Didier as he tapped on the open door and walked in.

Jacques shifted in his seat. "Sit down," he said, indicating the empty place at the other side of the coffee table.

Didier sat down and placed a couple of pieces of paper in front of his colleague.

"The painting 'Child in the Park' was created by an American artist, William Morton-Cleave. That's a copy of the picture." Didier handed Jacques a foolscap page with an image that almost covered the whole area.

Jacques took the printout and looked at the artwork. The colour palette was sparse, and the composition contained only two figures: a woman sitting on a bench at the furthest edge of the middle distance, and a child in a bonnet and white dress at the furthest edge of the foreground. Jacques shook his head and let out a small gasp.

"All this reading, Didier. I'm starting to think like a painter! So, when I look at this image, I immediately think about the picture's focus. It's hard to know if the artist wants us to consider the figures first, put the child before the woman, or perhaps pay more attention to the path the child is standing on or the substantial stone-built wall that dominates the left of the painting?" Jacques turned to look at his colleague. "And which is it?"

"It's the wall and the light and dark of the stones that were the artist's primary reason for creating the canvas, according to the information I've found on the internet."

"And what have you discovered about Morton-Cleave?"

Didier referred to his notes. "He was born into a wealthy New York family in 1849. The actual date is in the notes on the second page." He nodded towards the paper on the coffee table. "He travelled in Europe as a young man, mostly Germany and Italy, but there is nothing, so far, to indicate that he ever met Vallade. He was also a teacher, and he founded a school for artists in New York and often taught a summer school in Germany when he was in his thirties and forties. In America, Morton-Cleave is, alongside his contemporary William Merrit Chase, considered to be impressionistic in style and composition. In the States he is often referred to as an Impressionist. He is known for his New York cityscapes and more rural landscapes along the coast near his villa in the state of Vermont."

"And what about this particular painting? Do we know who owns it? Where it might be now? Anything?"

"I'm still following up on that lead. The exhibition mentioned in the notes on the page from the catalogue took place in New York in 1929 under the title of 'Exhibition for Impressionism across Europe and North America'. I haven't managed to get a composite list of all the exhibits yet." Didier sat back. "I'm waiting for a response from the archivist about a copy of the exhibition catalogue from 1929. The information about who loaned or gifted this painting, and the one we are interested in finding, is still unavailable. They need time to search their records before they can supply the further information."

Jacques nodded. "OK. Have they given any indication of how long that might take?"

Didier shook his head. "The person I spoke to gave me a long explanation about how difficult access to the archives was, how difficult it might be to find anything, and that when they undertake the search, they might not find anything relevant at all."

"Which means it could be?"

"A few days or a month or more. It was the best I could get the archivist to agree to." Didier shrugged.

"Alright." Jacques sat back on the sofa, his brow furrowed at the realisation that paying another visit to the library could not be avoided. *I hope that rude woman isn't there again.* "So, we keep on searching. At least we know there was a bona fide exhibition in 1929 that included the painting we are seeking. The exhibition was at a reputable establishment, so we can assume that the actual picture was intended to be there."

"But that's all at the moment," agreed Didier.

Jacques grimaced. "As we don't seem to be making much progress, perhaps it's a good thing that Madame ? hasn't fulfilled her commitment on the daily updates she said she wanted."

"Are you worried about that, Jacques?"

"Not really. I'm just starting to be concerned." He ran his hand over his chin, and the first indications of his five-o'clock shadow scratched at the skin of his fingers. "No," he said. "Concerned is the wrong word. I'm becoming suspicious."

"We could force the issue," said Didier. "We could say we have something that would encourage her to get in touch. Something to flush her out, perhaps."

"We've nothing to tell her, so what are you suggesting?"

"A message on our social media sites. All we need to say is that the artwork has been found and please contact us to arrange collection or for further details."

Jacques frowned. "Alright, that is a possibility. But we don't know how many other people Madame ? is involved with, nor who she has spoken to about this commission. We may be alerting the wrong person or people. And it's not actually truthful, is it?"

"You're right, but we both have a growing list of questions for her. She hasn't made contact as she said she would, and I think we've got to do something to get her attention."

Jacques remained silent as he thought through his colleague's suggestion.

"There are too many unanswered questions," continued Didier. "And, like you, I don't believe Madame ? has been completely honest with us."

"OK, Didier, get Maxim to put out a message that progress has been made on locating the painting. Further details can be obtained by contacting us, and use only the general office number and email, not our personal ones. I don't want to give the impression that we physically have the picture in our possession just in case it attracts interest from the wrong people."

"We'll get that out straight away. And do we continue working on the other aspects of the case, or do we wait?"

Jacques sighed and glanced across the room, his focus finally coming to rest on the floor-to-ceiling windows opposite.

"We continue the work," he said eventually. "We continue, and we wait and see what transpires." Jacques glanced at his watch. "Thanks, and I think I will continue my research at home."

Didier smiled and got up. "If I get anything else, I'll let you know," he said.

"One last thing, Didier, before you go. Monsieur Sforza. I know it's a new commission, but have we anything useful yet? It's just that Alain was here earlier, and he made it quite clear that he is very reticent to trust his potential client."

"Maxim and I have run lookup searches, and we are gradually working through all the results now."

"OK. Let me know if you find anything. Alain has asked for a forensic background check, so we need to examine everything in minute detail."

Didier nodded and headed for the door.

wednesday, june 5th, 08.06

Jacques strolled into place Chaptal, which was already buzzing with shoppers and traders behind their makeshift shop-fronts. Taking a tour around all the stalls, he occasionally stopped to look at something to give the impression that he had come to shop. At the *coutelier*, he paused and examined a penknife. Having made an entire circuit of the square and all the vendors, he took up a post in a small ginnel that allowed him to look onto the market without being too obvious about his need to watch who came and went.

He pulled out his phone and scanned the notes he had made about the man selling the toy dog he'd seen at the *kermesse*. No one at the morning's market was selling the same item, and whilst two of the traders present fitted the description he had jotted down, neither of them was the man Jacques was seeking.

"If he's an opportunist, he might arrive later." Jacques glanced at his watch. If the trader with the odd accent were going to show up at all, it would probably be in the next hour or so.

Jacques watched and waited, and after about twenty minutes he walked along rue du Soubeyran, took a right down Jarretiére – one of the oldest streets in the city – before turning into place au Blé. The market was much busier here, but the produce was mostly fruit, vegetables, bread and cheese. A slow tour of all the stalls showed no sign of the seller he was hunting.

Jacques slowly circled back through the shoppers. *Just in case I missed something.* He hadn't, and when he reached the top of the square he made his way back to place Chaptal. A final tour of this section of the market indicated there had been no new arrivals.

Checking his watch, he walked the length of the basilica, crossed place Urbain V, and made his way back to the office.

As he climbed the stairs to the fourth floor, he consoled himself with the assumption that the man would probably prefer the Saturday market because it was larger and busier, and therefore easier for him to slip in and set up his small table without being too noticeable.

Jacques crossed to his desk and began to unpack his bag, which he'd just dumped on his chair after dropping Lucien at Amélie's. With everything in its place, he sat down and, as always, scanned the information on the whiteboard. He smiled as he noted that the outstanding invoice had finally been paid by credit card over the phone that morning. It wasn't a great deal of money, but it was still needed to cover already-incurred expenses and provide a small profit for the business as a whole.

Underneath the listed cases was a note from Maxim in capital letters: MARIE ROUVIÈRE, and a file reference for the shared drive. Jacques logged in, opened the file and read the details. All factual and crafted using the minimum number of words. Jacques grinned. *Maxim, you would have made an excellent policeman.*

Clicking one of the links, he found himself on Madame Rouvière's business page listing. He scanned her career history, noting that her current post was as a lecturer at the College of Art in Paris.

"A daughter following in her father's footsteps."

Jacques pulled out his phone and dialled the number for the college that Maxim had included in the notes.

"I'd like to speak to Madame Marie Rouvière," he said once the phone had been answered at the other end of the line. "My name is Jacques Forêt, and I would like to discuss the catalogue of Vallade's art that her father compiled... No, I'm afraid that is impossible as I am not resident in Paris. Any discussion would have to be by video-link or across the internet." Jacques waited and listened, straining to hear and make sense of the whispered conversation in the background. Finally, the voice at the other end of the line became audible. "... Friday at three. That will be perfect, Madame. I will call you if you can give me the number to use... OK," he said as he jotted down the digits. "I'll call again on Friday, thank you."

With another lead to follow in play, Jacques settled down with the book on art and his ever-growing pages of notes.

EARLY TRAVELS IN FRANCE AND ITALY: 1907-1910

There are three of us now. Arturo has invited his friend Giancarlo to join us. He's arriving tomorrow. I've seen Gianni's work and I know I can learn a lot from him...

...Gianni is captivating. His work is all-encompassing. He's christened us the Circolo dei Pittori. I've never worked with such a frenzy, such energy. This will be my last letter for a while as we're packing and heading for the Limousin in two days' time.
—Charles-Marcel Vallade, 1908

With Giancarlo Abano and Arturo Fabbri, both students, Vallade began his travels through France and Italy. Neither Abano nor Fabbri would ever achieve the body of work that Vallade completed. But like Vallade, they would be overlooked, and their respective talents denigrated, for the early part of their careers.

The trio gradually moved south through the Limousin and then cross-country to Toulouse and Nîmes, down to the south coast to spend some time in Marseille and Aix-en-Provence before crossing the border into northern Italy and finally spending almost a year in Rome.

Again there are very few letters during this time, and even though Vallade became well-established during his time in Rome, he rarely wrote of his success. All three of the artists lived in communes or with each other's friends and relatives, earning what they could by selling their work.

Whilst in Rome Vallade met Vicontessa Lucrezia Santini, who became his model and his lover. It was whilst he was in Rome that he began painting portraits for the first time, the Vicontessa often being the subject. A full-length portrait of Lucrezia wearing a black and white dress set against a plain backdrop became the centrepiece of an exhibition that ran for a month in the city, and finally established Vallade as a painter of note.

The exhibition also included some of his early land- and seascapes, and over the next pages I will demonstrate how his use of light, fragmented light, and colour developed during this time.

mazargues in the 9th, wednesday, may 8th, 09.49

Madame Sorina Roșu turned into boulevard des Anges. She was late again, and it hadn't been her intention to be so. But her neighbour had kept her talking on avenue de la Soude, and it had been a struggle to get away. At the third attempt to extricate herself, Madame Roșu had succeeded, and now she was walking as fast as her floor-length skirt and petticoat would let her. A gust of wind channelled down the narrow street, dislodging her headscarf. She quickly pulled it forward again.

Fumbling for her keys in the pocket of her overall, she kept up her pace as the clock on the church flanking the dead-end of the street began to chime the new hour.

"Ah, not quite so late," she muttered to herself in her own language. French was a tongue she was still coming to terms with in her country of choice for residence. Her daughter was trying to help Madame Roșu improve her French by repeating words and phrases and translating them into their shared first language. But the older woman's attention to these lessons was thin at the best of times, and her memory – like that of many women of a certain age – was better on some days than others. It was just that those better days rarely, if ever, seemed to coincide with the language lessons.

Halfway down the street, set back a little from the road, was a small two-storey modern building with room for half a dozen cars to park outside in what was once the garden of a much older property that used to sit there. The former building, a small but unconventional-looking family home dating from the 1800s that had once belonged to an artist, had been demolished in the mid-seventies to make way for the newer development.

Madame Roşu and her skirts rustled into the compact parking area, keys in her hand, on the last stroke of ten. She let out a breath of relief. *Not late after all.* At the main entrance, she keyed in the code and stepped inside. Gathering a handful of her clothing, she climbed the stairs to the first floor. Unit B1 was her destination, and she slotted the key in the lock at the door and turned it.

"*Bonjour*," she shouted as she entered. The greeting was one of the few universal pieces of French vocabulary with which she had become familiar. It also alerted her employer, who might be in the small room at the back, that she was arriving to undertake her role as the cleaner.

Today was a good day for French. After almost three months of working in her current post, Madame Roşu now had the question of whether her position as cleaner was permanent or not, and she had the vocabulary fixed in her mind. She'd been muttering the sentence to herself since she had left her daughter's apartment in the ninth to walk to her workplace. Despite the interruption from her neighbour on the street, she had rehearsed the sentence all the way up the boulevard.

In the studio, her greeting went unanswered as she came through the door, which wasn't unusual. The door clicked shut behind Madame Roşu as she dropped her keys back into her pocket and then placed her basket on the floor. Her light but well-worn jacket was quickly shrugged off her shoulders and hung up on one of the pegs by the door. The only other item of clothing was a paint-splattered voluminous smock that her employer used when she was working on a canvas.

"Not here," Sorina muttered to herself. Her smile of satisfaction soon disintegrated into a severe frown as she mentally rehearsed her important sentence in French for the umpteenth time.

She went through the studio space to a door at the back that had been left slightly ajar. Inside was a small kitchen area, a full-length cupboard, and another door leading to a small toilet and washbasin. Collecting her cleaning materials and equipment from the closet, Madame Roşu set about her tasks.

An hour and a half later, with all surfaces in the kitchen and toilet area scrubbed and spotless, the floor mopped and shining, and the bank of four windows and the floor of the studio space equally clean and sparkling, Madame Roşu prepared to take her leave.

As she skirted the bank of cabinets that sat opposite the wall of windows at the front of the room, she noticed that the expected envelope containing her payment wasn't in its usual place. The envelope with her name on it was always left on top of one of the large cabinets.

Madame Roşu shook her head. "No money today!"

This particular section of the studio, like the easels, was not to be touched. Ever. Her employer had made that absolutely clear right from the outset to her daughter, who had translated the instruction. She glanced down to see if the envelope might have fallen.

"Ah," she admonished herself. "You've just finished the floor. You would have seen it." And had that been the case, Madame Roşu would have picked up the envelope, put it back where it should have been, and then finished her task. She would never take payment for work she had not fully completed. She gazed around the light and airy space as a realisation began to form in her mind. Everything in the studio had been immaculate. She glanced at the cabinets with their shelves of paints and equipment.

"Everything looks the same as when I left last week," she muttered.

Another thought struck her. Had she somehow upset her employer to such an extent that another cleaner had been employed? Was that why everything had been so tidy? Casting her mind back to her previous visit on the morning of the first of the month, she mentally worked through the tasks for that day. Not that they were notably any different from today. It was then that she remembered the large tube of paint that had been left without its cap on the draining board in the kitchen, and the massive brownish-red stain in the sink that she had had to scrub and scrub at to remove.

"I shouldn't have moved the paint. No, I shouldn't have done that." She glanced around anxiously, scanning the cabinet shelves and looking for where she had left the tube. But it was precisely where she had put it the previous week. The fact that it was still there was evidence enough, as far as Madame Roşu was concerned, that she had done no wrong after all.

"But I better not do that again," she told herself.

Confused, Madame Roşu stared at the covered easels in the centre of the space, wondering what to do, questioning if the tall static tripods would provide an answer. The dingy white sheets of material made her think of paper. "A note. If I can find a piece of paper, I can leave a note." She moved to the cabinet that contained trays and shelves of all kinds of paper and all sorts of artist's equipment, and many other things she didn't recognise.

"But what would I write?" Madame Roşu slowly turned around looking for inspiration.

"My important question," she muttered. But, as soon as the words were uttered and the rehearsed French popped into her mind, she dismissed it. Whilst a note about the longevity of her job was necessary, it didn't address the issue of her lack of pay for that morning's work. And how would she write a sentence about that without Elena to help her? Moving further along the shelves, she gingerly pulled out one or two of the trays.

"No, I can't touch any of this stuff," she said as she pushed the trays back into place. She sighed. Resigned to leaving without being paid, she walked to the door.

"I'll talk to Elena," she decided. "My daughter will know what to do when she comes home from work this evening."

With that thought fixed in her head, Sorina pulled on her jacket. She picked up her basket and wondered if her employer might have decided to leave her money for the morning's work at the house with her Friday money.

"Ah, that would be easier for her. That's what she's done," she persuaded herself as she pulled open the door, let herself out, and locked up. Happy with her new interpretation of what had transpired, Madame Roşu pocketed her keys and left.

mende, wednesday, june 5th, 14.03

Didier called into the small gallery on rue du Soubeyran. He'd known it had been there for quite a while, but he had never been in before. The front door was propped open to allow the light and some air from the gentle breeze to circulate around the old beamed property. The shop was narrow at the front, with barely room for the doorway and a similar width of window, but it extended right to the back of the building.

A small counter took up one corner of the space behind the window display – a small but carefully-arranged selection of cards and a couple of pictures. On the wall behind the counter were other framed artworks: some watercolours and one or two in oils. On the other two walls were cards of all kinds, a small selection of art supplies, and some ready-made standard-sized frames and mounts. In the far corner were a set of narrow wooden stairs with a sign on the wall stating *Gallery*.

Didier hesitated. The silence in the shop and the quiet attention of the lady behind the counter made him reticent to take the stairs.

"Madame, *bonjour*, is the gallery open?" Didier noticed that her name badge claimed she was called Henriette.

"Monsieur. Yes, the gallery is open," she smiled. "Please go up. The artworks are spread across all three floors."

Didier nodded and slowly climbed, the wooden treads creaking and groaning with the individual note of each step as it took his weight. The corner was so dark he wondered why a sensor had not been fitted so that the light on the landing would come on automatically as soon as someone trod on the first stair. But some of the oldest buildings – those that had not crumbled, been renovated or deliberately destroyed and replaced – were in this part of the city. As he moved up the flight, the light from the first floor became more visible and gradually spilt out onto the landing and the top three or four steps.

This room was much airier and brighter. The white blinds covering the windows protected the artworks from the sun but still allowed the pictures to be illuminated. He slowly moved around the four walls, looking at each item. One or two had *SOLD* stickers attached to one corner of the frame, but the rest carried small neat price tags.

The display seemed to have no rhyme, reason, or connecting theme. A picture of poppies in a field in oils sat next to a seascape in watercolour, which in turn abutted a charcoal sketch of the local *Aubrac* cattle in a mountain pasture. For this one, he studied and read the small explanatory card at the side.

"A local artist, then," he muttered.

Having spent the morning undertaking a complete security evaluation of a large property on the city's outskirts, Didier couldn't stop himself from checking out the arrangements within the gallery. His gaze shifted to the top corners of the room, and he nodded his approval.

"CCTV," he muttered. "And it looks modern and sophisticated."

Moving across to the narrow staircase, he went up to the second floor. The room was of the same size and design as the previous one, and a glance up to the ceiling corners confirmed that CCTV was also present. He moved around this display more quickly, noting the same eclectic style of presentation.

Mounting the final flight to the third level in the gallery, he paused on the top step. As with the other rooms, the walls contained most of the work for viewing. But in the centre of this space were several easels arranged in a hexagon. The picture that first caught his eye made him gasp for breath. In an ornate gilt frame was an image with the title *Sunday Afternoon on the Beach*. Didier stared at it.

"No, I'm wrong. That's not the right picture. It can't be."

He moved closer, and squatting down on one knee, he put his briefcase at the foot of the stand and pulled out his paper copy of the picture they had been commissioned to find.

Standing again, he held out the sheet of paper at the side of the painting. Looking from one to the other, he noted the similarities and the differences.

"It appears to be the same picture… But then it's not," he said, to no one in particular. He grabbed his phone from the top pocket of his shirt and took a photo.

Turning away from the arrangement of tripods in the centre of the space, he looked at the displays along the walls. The pictures were interspersed with information panels, the first of which gave a short history of the life of Charles-Marcel Vallade. Didier looked at two oils and a watercolour and moved on to the following information board. He continued around the room, taking photos on his phone.

Finally, turning back to the six easels in the centre, he systematically captured photos of all of the remaining artworks. At the sixth, he stopped and stared. For a moment, the image fixed him to the spot.

Recovering himself, he scrolled through his contact list and dialled the selected number.

"Jacques, it's me… I'm in the gallery on rue du Soubeyran. It's just behind the basilica. You need to see this… I'm on the third floor… As quick as you can."

***

On the ground floor, the shop assistant Henriette had been changing and re-arranging some of the greetings cards on display. It was only as she turned to take some new cards out of one of the drawers below the counter that she noticed the behaviour of her only customer up on the third floor.

"What are you up to?" She watched as the man made a call. "And who are you calling?" Pulling her bag out of the bottom drawer, she searched inside for her phone.

She looked at the monitor. The customer was standing in

the centre of the room, seemingly transfixed by one of the Vallade oils. She dialled.

"Agnès, there's something strange happening... A man up on the third floor is taking photos on his phone of all the Vallades... Yes, I think you should get here quickly... Don't know... OK. See you soon."

Henriette slipped her phone back into her bag and watched the monitor.

***

Jacques ran down the stairs two at a time. In a moment he was out of the office building and sprinting along boulevard Théophile Roussel. He cut into place Urbain V, raced across to Soubeyran and stood outside the shop for a moment to get his breath back.

"Madame, *bonjour*," he said as he strolled across the threshold. "May I visit the gallery?"

"Of course, the stairs are over there."

Jacques smiled, moved across the room, and bounded up the three flights of stairs. As he emerged onto the landing on the third floor, he stopped and looked around the space.

"So, all of these are Vallades?"

Didier nodded. "But this is the most interesting one," he said as he stepped back from the easel.

Jacques walked around to the far side of the display. He reached into his jacket pocket to pull out his copy of the image of the lost painting, but stopped as Didier held up his version at the side of the large ornate frame.

Jacques looked from one version of the picture to the other, making mental comparisons. "That's our artwork," he said, turning his attention to the small information board at the other side of the painting. "That is the picture."

"No it's not," came a mature female voice from somewhere on the other side of the room.

Jacques and Didier moved out from behind the display.

"Ah, Madame," said Jacques as he walked across to the landing. "I was wondering when and how you would get in touch and ask for an update." Jacques turned to Didier.

"This is our client. Madame, this is my colleague Didier Duclos. Perhaps you could introduce yourself properly, now."

The woman stepped forward and removed her sunglasses. "Agnès Fribourg," she said, holding out her hand for Didier to take.

"*Enchanté*, Madame."

Wearing a forced smile, Jacques stood with his feet apart and his hands on his hips.

"I think you owe us an explanation, Madame Fribourg. And it had better be a good one."

wednesday, june 5th, 15.32

Jacques, Didier and Madame Fribourg were sitting hunched around a small circular table used as a desk in a small office behind the shop on the ground floor of the gallery. In the corner of the room stood an easel supporting the Vallade painting they had been commissioned to find.

"That is not my painting," Madame Fribourg said.

"Let's start at the beginning," said Jacques, pulling out his notebook. "Now that I know this place is here, let's begin with the shop, the gallery, this painting, and, perhaps most importantly, YOU, Madame. Who are you really?"

Madame Fribourg attempted a smile, but it failed, and she quickly looked away, her eyes darting about the room.

"Madame…?" Jacques prompted and waited.

"Yes, I suppose I do owe you some sort of explain—"

"No!" Jacques' tone was thunderous. "You owe us only the right explanation, Madame. The truthful one."

"I am who I say I am," she whispered.

"*Carte d'Identité*," demanded Jacques. "If you don't mind," he added as an after-thought.

"Of course." Madame Fribourg delved into her bag, pulled out her purse and opened the section for notes at the window that showed her ID card. She handed it over. Jacques glanced at the photo and passed the card to Didier.

"Note all the details, please. A name means nothing, Madame, so we will be checking your ID," he said, looking Madame Fribourg in the eye. Meanwhile, Didier removed the card from its pocket and captured the information on his phone before handing the purse back.

"I see from your ID that you were born in Marseille. So why are you here in Mende?"

"My husband was born here. He was an artist, and I

stayed after he died because I had the gallery and the shop, my home, and I wanted to remain here."

"The local sketches in the displays downstairs," said Didier. "Are they your husband's?"

Madame Fribourg smiled. "Yes. His landscapes were popular with local people, but his sketches and watercolours always sold well to the tourists in the summer. And they continue to do so now as prints."

"So, you own the gallery and this property?"

"Yes and no, Monsieur Forêt. Yes, I own the business, but the property is on a long lease, and the charges are paid annually."

"And the tribute to Vallade? What's that about?"

Madame Fribourg looked up at the painting on the easel. "That child is my mother, and the woman in the pink and white dress holding the white parasol is my grandmother. But that is not my painting."

Jacques turned to look at the artwork. He frowned. It looked exactly like the painting he'd been asked to recover.

"If that isn't yours, it must be either an authorised copy or a forgery. Which is it, Madame?"

Madame Fribourg grinned. "You've been doing your homework, Monsieur Forêt. There are no authorised copies of that picture. The canvas in that frame is a forgery."

"You seem very certain of that," said Didier.

"I am, Monsieur Duclos," she said. "I am absolutely convinced that the picture I have is a forgery. The work is extremely well done, of course. But it is not the original."

Jacques glanced at his colleague. *Do we believe her or not?*

"Messieurs," she continued, folding her arms across her chest and looking from one to the other. "I'm sixty-nine years old, and I have lived with that painting all my life. I know every brushstroke. Every nuance of colour. I know it like I know my own skin."

Jacques tapped his pen against his notebook. "Alright, let's accept that it is a forgery. If the painting has been in your possession constantly, then at some point, it must have been exchanged for the real one. Can you pinpoint when that might have happened?"

"I've spent almost every waking moment thinking about that since I first noticed it was a forgery."

"And when was that?"

Madame Fribourg opened her mouth to speak, let out a breath and shook her head. "There's something I need to explain to you first."

"Go on," said Jacques.

"The original painting is mine. I inherited it from my mother, who inherited it from my grandmother. It is wholly and legally mine. My grandmother was given the original by Vallade himself, long before I was born. When he first became ill, he formed a Trust to oversee his work and his estate. He knew he was unlikely to outlive cancer. When he died in 1972, the Trust oversaw his estate, and they contested the gift. But my grandmother had letters, and it was quite clear what Vallade's intentions were. But the Trust's lawyer was very skilled, extremely adept, and probably very expensive." She shrugged. "We lost the fight. Although we would retain ownership, we were instructed to make the painting available for the public to view. It was agreed that we would have it from May first until the end of October, and from *Toussaint* until April thirtieth it would be with the Trust."

"Which means that the copying and exchange could have taken place at any point between those dates since the sharing arrangement was agreed and put into place," said Didier.

"Not quite," said Madame Fribourg. "The sharing arrangement began in May 1975, and my mother took detailed photographs of every centimetre of the artwork, the stretcher, the frame. Everything, both front and back. I have those images and later images as digital copies, which I use for comparison every time the picture moves. I noticed it had been exchanged for the forgery when it arrived here in May. I saw it instantly." Madame Fribourg smiled. "There are some things you never ever forget, Monsieur Forêt. In a certain light and from a certain angle, the brushstrokes in the bottom left corner of the painting make the shape of a small golden galleon sinking beneath the sand. That used to mesmerise me as a child." She grinned. "For quite a while, I couldn't understand why the ship was there sometimes but not others. I thought it was magic. The light is usually right where the picture sits up in the gallery in the early afternoon, and if I get down on the floor, I can still see the optical illusion. It's always my very last check. In the past, it has often been my only check."

Jacques flicked back through his notes. "And that was when you called us the first time."

Madame Fribourg nodded.

Didier shook his head as he glanced at the floor. "You didn't think about reporting the theft to the police," he said, looking Madame in the eye. "Any particular reason for that?"

"I had a forgery in my possession, Monsieur Duclos! How would that look?" She sighed and pulled her fingers through the hair tucked behind her right ear. "I believed I would have a tough time convincing the police that it – the actual painting – really was missing," she said in a more measured tone. "I was also very concerned about any taint that a police investigation might bring to the gallery and to the picture itself."

"OK," said Jacques. "This changes the whole investigation. How is the picture moved from here to… the Trust?"

"A privately-owned removal company collect it and deliver it to the Vallade Museum in Finistère. The Trust manages the museum, and the picture is displayed there and brought back by the same carrier six months later." Madam Fribourg opened her purse, pulled out a business card, and pushed it across the table to Jacques.

"Thank you. We will check out the courier. It's possible they could be involved in facilitating the exchange of your picture."

Madame Fribourg shook her head. "I don't think so. If

anyone is behind this, it will be the Trust. The Trust tried to get possession of my artwork in 1972, and they've been trying ever since with their requests for extended loan periods and requests for loans to other exhibitions. I've refused every one of them."

"We will be contacting the Trust as well, Madame." Jacques glanced at his watch and turned to Didier. "I need to go. Lucien will be back at the office. Can you finish up here please, and undertake a security check of this building, too?" Jacques stood and pocketed his notebook.

"A security check? Is that necessary, Monsieur?"

"Yes, Madame, it is. I know you believe the Trust is behind the exchange, but I have to look at every possibility. Sometimes just to rule them out. But everything has to be considered."

"As you wish."

"I'll see you at the office tomorrow," he said to Didier. "Madame, excuse me, I have a young son who will be waiting for me. I will be in touch as we make progress with your case."

Jacques squeezed through the confined space and out into the central area of the shop floor. The lady at the counter was busy with a customer, and Jacques quietly slipped out and made his way to his own office.

wednesday, june 5th, 16.45

As Jacques walked into the main office, he could hear the children's voices, Lucien's being the loudest. Amélie was supervising a story-telling game.

"Everything alright?" Jacques peered around the corner of the screen, and Lucien immediately jumped up.

"Look at my picture, *Papa*." He stood pointing to a landscape affixed to the play area wall that looked very much like the view from the loft at the chalet in Messandrierre.

I seem to be surrounded by landscapes. "Very good. Will you stay with everyone else until the end of your story, or come with me?"

Lucien grinned. "Here," he announced and plopped back down on his beanbag to continue the game.

Jacques smiled at Amélie. "I think that's a definite no," he said. "Amélie, I'd like to have a word with you when you can find a moment, please."

"I'll finish this game and then come through. Maxim will look after the children."

"Thanks," said Jacques, turning to move to Maxim's desk. "Our work on the missing painting has just become more complex. Would you like to come through and bring any notes or updates with you, please?"

Maxim stood and followed Jacques to his office. "I've got a message for you to ring a Madame Taillard. She said you already have her number."

Jacques sat at his desk. "Thanks, and yes, I do." He scribbled a note, deciding no further explanation was required.

Maxim hesitated. "OK," he said eventually. "I think I've got a handle on the newspaper article and what it might refer to." Maxim placed the scrap of newsprint on the desk. "It's about the settlement of a will. I should have a full copy of that in the next day or so."

"This is Charles-Marcel Vallade's will?"

"Yes, but the issue surrounds a codicil that was added to the original at the beginning of 1961. The content of the first version of the will is not affected."

"I wouldn't be too sure about that. A codicil usually means that something indirectly referred to in the will becomes specific and attracts its own importance. Arguments begin because of others' long-held expectations. Let me know as soon as you get that copy."

Maxim nodded. "The second issue is about the painting. I can't find anything about it other than the exhibition in New York and the references to it in the catalogue listing all Vallade's works. There are no mentions of sales or auctions."

"Which would support Madame Fribourg's contention that the painting was a gift and has been in her family for three generations," muttered Jacques as he stared at the whiteboard.

Maxim frowned. "Madame Fribourg?"

"What? Oh yes, sorry, Maxim. I have an update of my own." He got up, picked up a marker from his desk and went to the whiteboard.

"Our client now has a name," he said, scrubbing out the original note with a scruffy cloth and writing *Agnès Fribourg* instead. "She lives here in Mende, and she owns the gallery and shop on rue du Soubeyran."

"Oh yes, I know where you mean. Amélie goes in there to get cards sometimes."

"The painting, Maxim? Anything else?"

"Only that I've also looked at the dark web, and there's a lot of chatter in various forums about parcels, packages or deliveries. From the context, it's clear they're valuable, but there's nothing specific. I haven't taken that any further."

"Thanks, Maxim. Didier and I have discovered today that the painting has been exchanged for a forgery, which is currently in Madame Fribourg's possession rather than the original. I have some extra tasks for you. Can you run a full profile search on Madame Fribourg, please? Didier has the details from her *Carte d'Identité* on his phone. Check her social media, everything. Can you check the details of her marriage, too? Her husband was also an artist and died a few years ago."

"I'll get onto the archives. How far back do you want me to go?"

Jacques ran through the recent conversation about the painting in his head. *What was it she said?* A smile of recognition crossed his face. "Go back to her mother and her parentage."

"OK." Maxim made a note.

With a deep frown on his face, Jacques searched his mind for another fact that he knew he had picked up during the conversation at the gallery. "Sixty-nine," he said. He looked at Maxim. "Madame Fribourg said she was sixty-nine years of age, so that would put the year of her birth as 1949 or 1950. Didier will have the full date of birth on his phone. And she was born in Marseille."

"OK. I'll get Didier to send me the pics of the ID card so that I can set the initial searches running. When he comes in tomorrow, I should be able to identify what looks relevant."

"Good. The last thing is that this case is no longer about finding a painting. It's also about finding the forger. It is most important that we keep everything confidential, Maxim."

Maxim nodded. "I won't mention anything to Amélie, then."

"And I think we need to ensure we do not discuss this case in the main office when the children are here after school. Similarly, with phone calls, make them from this room if I'm not in or from the small storeroom opposite."

"Sure. Anything else, Jacques?"

"No, that's everything, thanks."

As Maxim turned and left, Jacques picked up his mobile and scrolled through his long list of contacts until he found an old colleague from his time in Paris. He stopped and looked up.

"It's been twelve years." He glanced at his phone and then put it down on the desk. Signing into his laptop, he went straight to Facebook and logged in. In the search box, he typed in *Zahid Toumi*. The first few options didn't look right, but then he came to a *Zahid the Collector* in Paris, with a profile picture of an antique clock.

"That's you, Zahid. I'd stake my life on it." He checked the profile and the timeline, and then searched the *Friends* list for a couple of names of other officers they had both served with. "That's definitely you." Jacques quickly typed out a direct message. All he had to do now was wait.

Almost as soon as Maxim had left, Amélie walked in.

"Jacques, you said you wanted a chat. Is now a good time?"

"Of course, come in, sit down, and don't look so worried. What I want to talk to you about could be advantageous if you're interested."

Amélie smiled and relaxed back into the chair. "Oh, OK."

"I was talking to Alain from the Vaux Group a little earlier, and he has come up with a proposition that might interest you. He wants to create an on-site *crêche* for all parents in the Vaux organisation in some vacant rooms in this building. He suggested that we might take on that space, and, therefore, responsibility for the facility. Of course, it would mean that Lucien and your two children could use it rather than the space in the main office. Alain also wondered if you would be interested in working in the new area, either as a member of the childcare team or as the manager. He's offering an hourly rate of two per cent above the standard."

"I suppose Alain thinks I would work full-time as the manager?"

"It's possible, but nothing is final yet. The area needs to be refitted, and the facility, once it is running, will need to pay for itself." Jacques looked at her, wondering what was going through her head. He certainly couldn't read her face.

"Can I think about it and let you know?"

"Of course," said Jacques. "Take as long as you need, and..." He was about to say that he thought she should discuss it with Maxim, but something about the direct gaze she had turned on him put the idea out of his mind. "Let me know your thoughts as soon as you're ready," he said.

Amélie gave the slightest of nods and got up. "I'll let you know before the end of the week," she said as she turned and went to the door. "Thanks for the offer." She pulled the door closed behind her.

Jacques stared at the rectangle of light brown wood as though it were a deliberately-placed immovable barrier.

"I think Alain is going to be disappointed." He turned his attention to his notes and research, and a bizarre thought ran through his mind. *Of course, a refusal might be what Alain intended all along.*

wednesday, june 5th, 21.18

With a cold beer and the book on art, Jacques resumed his research on the life and work of Vallade. The warm evening air had become oppressive, and Jacques had retreated into the cool of the *salon*. The air conditioning lightly hummed in the background.

Jacques stretched himself out on the sofa, the baby monitor on the coffee table echoing Lucien's contented sleep. He put his phone on the table and picked up the book. Not bothering to go to the last page he had read, he immediately turned to the index of paintings at the back. Running his finger down the column and on the fourth page, he found *Sunday Afternoon on the Beach* listed at page 148. He quickly leafed through the book, only to find that if he'd read for a little longer the previous evening, he would have reached that page before being called to the gallery.

Setting the book down flat on the table, he studied the image, which stretched the entire width of the top two-thirds of the page. He let his gaze rove across the scene, the colours and the grouping of the figures. For some reason, the artwork looked brighter; the colours seemed more vibrant. Placing the copy of the image that Madame Fribourg had given him when she first summoned him to the parking area on the col, he was surprised to see how different the colour palette was between the two versions. *At least two or three shades different.*

He looked up for a moment. "Where did that knowledge come from?" He turned in response to what he thought was a shadow. But there was nothing there.

The two images commanded his attention. "Two shades different. Definitely two." *How do I suddenly know that?* He took a sip of his beer and decided that he should concentrate.

Focussing on the listing beneath the image in the book, he started to read.

Sunday Afternoon on the Beach ca. 1921

Oil on canvas 61.6 x 88.9cm (24¼ x 35 in)
Signed: C-MV (l.-r.)

Private collection

As he was about to begin reading the detailed explanation for the painting, his phone rang. It was his ex-colleague Zahid Toumi. Jacques picked up the call immediately.

"Zahid, good to hear from you, and thanks for calling back… I'm very well, thank you, and I have my own private investigation business, a son, and I'm living here in the Cévennes. What about you?"

Jacques listened as his old friend quickly brought him up to date.

"Yes, you're right. I have a specific reason for getting in touch …"

Jacques laughed. "That's not true, and you know it. I'm calling you because I need some help with art fraud, and you're the best man for the job… Join my team? No, I don't think that will be necessary. As much as I would be happy to work with you again, I probably can't afford your fees! But if you could spare us about an hour or so tomorrow or the day after to answer some questions and talk us through some basics, that would help a great deal… It will be me, my partner Didier Duclos, and Maxim, who manages our admin and is our internet and social media wizard… Great, thanks, Zahid. Ten tomorrow and we'll call you… Yes … *À demain*."

The next link in place, Jacques settled back with the art and the life of Charles-Marcel Vallade. He continued to read until almost one. Having devoured the detailed description of the painting, he went back to the beginning of the section and carried on, re-reading the paragraphs dedicated to *Sunday Afternoon on the Beach*. Then he turned to the remaining pages in that part of the book.

THE BRITTANY YEARS: 1911-1937

> *It's good to be back and with my beautiful wife. Of course, we're keeping the villa in Honfleur and the unconventional old house in the 9th – I got so much painting done when I was last there…*
> *I will come and see you soon, Maman, I promise.*
> —Charles-Marcel Vallade, 1925

The pre- and post-war years of the early twentieth century were very productive for Vallade. The portfolio of sketches and panels he had amassed during his travels provided plenty of material for full canvases which he then exhibited across the country as well as in Paris. But he still continued to add to his œuvre with numerous watercolours and oils of the familiar countryside of his native north-west France.

Whilst in Honfleur, in 1922 he met an American heiress with a taste for the work of the Impressionists and she very quickly developed a fascination for Vallade's work, actively promoting him to her society friends and relatives. He received a significant number of commissions for portraits and family groups throughout this time. He complained in a letter to his ageing stepmother that he *'felt confined and pallid'* because he was required to spend so much time indoors on the commissions.

In 1923 he married Charlotte Adella Rusholme-Knight, the wedding being the talk of all the American society magazines of the time. The couple spent most of the next two years in Paris, returning to Brittany for very short stays. When their son was born in the January of 1925, it was Charlotte who decided that they should return to the sprawling Bretagne estate and live there permanently.

Between 1925 and 1938, Vallade completed some of his most impressive seascapes and landscapes. He also took time to record his family life and often used his wife and son, along with models, household servants and estate personnel, and friends to create scenes. One such is **L178 *Sunday Afternoon on the Beach***.

During this period of his life, Vallade lost his stepmother. She had become frail, and a cold developed into pneumonia. Within a few days of the final diagnosis she was dead. Vallade was devastated.

L.178

Sunday Afternoon on the Beach ca. 1921

Oil on canvas 61.6 x 88.9cm (24¼ x 35 in)
Signed: C-MV (l.-r.)

Private collection

There are no auction or exhibition records for the present work. In concept and design it is very similar to *Côte d'Opale* (L.165) which was completed on panel. In both works Vallade uses a simple diagonal setting of a shore line as the backdrop for his cast of figures, mostly women and children. They are well-dressed and the poses are comfortably relaxed – perhaps a representation of Vallade's relatively new-found confidence as an artist and improved status, or possibly just a comment on the leisure class of the time.

What is particularly striking in this work is the recumbent young man in the foreground. This is long after Vallade stopped using his friends and fellow-artists as models. It was also around this time that he began to pay models to sit for him. Later, after he married, he would often use his family in scenes such as this.

In my view, this particular piece is about how the figures are integrated into the landscape and how they are arranged and juxtaposed, rather than a social comment. There are plenty of his later works that fit into that mould.

This picture is one of the earliest instances that I have been able to find that demonstrates his use of colour to create a route for the viewer's eye to travel through the scene. Here Vallade uses yellow to achieve that. Three years later he would use a particular shade of red, and maintain the use of that colour until the end of his life. The choice of the colour yellow in this scene makes it especially rare and therefore much more collectable. Every time I look at this picture I wonder what it might have made if Vallade had ever offered it for auction.

Sunday Afternoon on the Beach was gifted to one of his favoured models, who is said to be the woman seated in the bottom right quadrant. The child near her is likely her own, but, despite extensive searches, I can find no confirmation of this in any of his surviving letters.

thursday, june 6th, 08.04

Didier and Jacques had arrived early so they could catch up with each other and share information. Jacques was keen to understand how the security visit at the gallery on rue du Soubeyran had gone.

"The security system at the gallery is adequate, and the CCTV is set up to run during the day, but only when the gallery is open," said Didier with a look of incredulity on his face. "Staffing is sparse, and no curators are employed to be situated in each room as would be the case in a much larger gallery or a museum."

"What if a break-in occurred?" Jacques asked. "The alarm would be tripped, but would that automatically cause the CCTV to begin recording again?"

Didier shook his head. "No. It's set up completely independently of the alarm system, which was put in about thirty years ago when the gallery first opened. At that point, the display on the third floor was not in place."

"OK," said Jacques. "So, the CCTV is for giving an eye on the other rooms to the person behind the counter where the till is. And that's it?"

Didier nodded.

"And if they spotted someone on camera taking a picture from one of the walls... What would happen then? Does Madame Fribourg have a process in place for that eventuality?"

"There's a basic strategy in place. Whoever is on the counter at the time will lock the front door and call the *police municipale* immediately."

Jacques let out a gasp and shook his head in disbelief. "How can anyone be that naïve, Didier?" He shrugged. "Now I'm thinking about the insurance on that place. With valuable paintings on display, the insurance company would surely want better protection."

"That's something else that I think is very odd, Jacques. So odd that it made me very suspicious. The actual pictures themselves are not insured against theft, only against fire and damage."

"That doesn't make sense to me. Who are the underwriters?"

"That's where it gets even more complicated. The underwriters are the Trust that manages the Vallade estate, and the policy was specifically drawn up as it is."

"So, the executors of Vallade's estate are the owners of the pictures – is that what you mean?"

Didier looked blank. "I don't know, Jacques. I need to do some more digging, and we need a copy of the original will with all the bequests and settlements before I can answer that."

"Maxim has that in hand, but these paintings may belong to no one individual at the moment. They could belong wholly to the Vallade estate instead. Is that it?"

"Yes, it's possible."

"Something else, Didier. Do the shop or gallery keep recordings from the CCTV, and how regularly is it overwritten if they do?"

"It's on a weekly rotation."

"So today's recording will be overwritten by next week's recording on the same day?"

"That's right."

Jacques took a deep breath and drummed his fingers on the desk. "This is a strange set of arrangements," he said.

Didier nodded. "If those paintings were mine, or I was responsible for their security in any way, I'd be livid that the gallery was being so cavalier."

Jacques continued drumming his fingers. "Cavalier! It's such an odd set of circumstances that I'm starting to think something else might be behind it. Something sinister, and I'm wondering if some choices were made deliberately."

"But why would anyone deliberately put their valuable

possessions at risk like that?"

"Because they were persuaded to, or heavily encouraged to do so."

"I think you mean forced to, for some reason."

"Possibly. At the moment, my mind is crowded with all kinds of possibilities, Didier. We have the museum, we have the Trust, and we have Madame Fribourg and no apparent clear legal ownership. Although Madame Fribourg was adamant that the painting we are searching for was hers outright. Did she explain how and why that is the case?"

Didier shook his head. "No."

"OK. In the meantime, we have other avenues to follow. I will talk to the carriers. I also think we need to speak to any remaining members of the Vallade family and the people at the Trust, once Maxim has tracked down who is still around and where they are. It would also be interesting to know if the gallery here has ever reported a break-in or an attempted break-in, or if there are any reports of suspicious activity around the building. It might be useful to find out if the painting has ever been reported missing or stolen before."

"Maxim has already done an extensive search for the painting by name, and we are gradually working through all the references. So far, we've come up with a blank. I'll get on to those other issues later today."

"Thanks, Didier. And what about Alain's case? Where are we with that?"

"I've traced some businesses that Monsieur Sforza owns or is connected with. But I'm still waiting for the results of some searches to come to fruition. What we do know is that Milo Sforza lives in and around Marseille. He has a top-floor apartment in the first *arrondissement* and a substantial villa on the city's outskirts."

"Anything else, apart from the bank statements for closed accounts?"

"Not so far, but…"

"Go on, Didier."

"At the moment this is just a hunch, Jacques. It's the

range of businesses Sforza seems to be involved with that is making me suspicious. He has various properties in the city's northern quarter, which suggests drugs to me. The plot of land that Alain is selling is north of the city. I've requested the *plan cadastral* details so I can check the boundaries. But I can't help wondering if Alain's plot adjoins some of the plots that house Sforza's businesses."

"It's possible, and that would explain Sforza's immediacy in making an offer."

"I was thinking of heading down there to look at one or two of them to see what's going on."

"How urgent is this from Alain's point of view?"

"Not that urgent at the moment. At least two other buyers are interested, and Alain doesn't want to jump in immediately. He's had a couple of other enquiries, and he told me yesterday that one of those may bring forward an offer that will put Sforza out of the running."

"OK, maybe we can reconsider your visit to Marseille early next week."

"Agreed," said Didier.

Jacques glanced at his watch. "The video link with Zahid is coming up shortly. We'll use this room, but we must ensure that we all have our laptops positioned so Zahid can't see anything connected with our business in the background. He's an old work colleague, but he is still a serving detective, and we need to be careful we don't place ourselves or him in a difficult position. If you could brief Maxim, please."

Didier nodded and left.

thursday, june 6th, 10.03

The team gathered in Jacques' office. Maxim took a seat on the sofa with his laptop on the coffee table to the left of the room. Didier was sitting at the far side of Jacques' desk with his laptop where the old desktop used to be. Jacques was in his usual place with his computer in the centre of the desk. Only he had direct sight of the whiteboard with the details of their current cases.

Maxim was busy getting the video connections to work as he gradually linked all four of them into one conversation.

"Zahid, thanks for joining us, and these are my colleagues Didier Duclos and Maxim Arnoux." Jacques looked over towards his partner. *Do I tell Zahid we are recording this?* The moment the question formed in his mind, he knew the answer. *We will only be using the recording for our own reference.*

"I want to make clear that this is an off-the-record discussion. Are you OK with that?"

"As I said last night, Jacques, I'm on leave for the next few days, and I'm at home at the moment, and I'm happy to share my expertise with you as much as I can. But if you mention something that means I should properly take action, I may not be able to let that go. You know that as well as I do."

Jacques glanced at Didier, who nodded. When he turned to Maxim, he mouthed the word 'Understood'.

Jacques took a deep breath. "OK. We have a client who legally owns an oil painting. The painting was…" Jacques paused for a moment. "The painting was out on loan. When it was returned, the owner discovered that the original had been replaced with a forgery, and she has asked us to recover her picture."

Zahid grimaced. "It happens. Presumably there's an insurance company involved? It's not unusual for owners of high-value items to lend them out occasionally, then cry foul and claim reparation from the insurance company. Does that seem likely in this case?"

"No."

Zahid paused. "That suggests you're certain, Jacques."

"I am. I've seen the forgery, and to me, it looks exactly like the actual painting. It's something that someone has taken quite some time to create, I think."

"And it's not an authorised copy?"

"No. And according to my client, the painting has always been in the family's possession. It has never been offered for auction or had any form of copy authorised."

Zahid nodded. "You're right. Someone has gone to a lot of trouble. OK. There are two basic kinds of forgers, Jacques. The first group are just in the business for as much money as they can make, and are mostly connected with serious crime, such as human trafficking, drugs, and counterfeiting, to feed any of those forms of crime but also to create funds for it. In those spheres, the forgers are genuinely talented people in their own field who have often just been discovered by someone connected with the criminal gang. Once they've done one job, they become subsumed within that underground organisation. Sometimes by force."

The still silence in the room echoed the rapt interest of Zahid's listeners.

"The second group are something of a dying breed. These are also highly-talented people, and the vast majority are honest because they work as professional copyists for museums, galleries, private collectors, and other companies that create limited editions of paintings, prints and books. I say they are a dying breed because technology has overtaken their genuine work. It is possible to create a copy of an old master, for instance, using a high-resolution photograph and a specialist printer to copy the photo onto canvas. The canvas is then put on a stretcher and framed and sold. It's a legitimate business, Jacques, and galleries worldwide are doing it."

"Is it possible to tell a genuine hand-created copy from a digitally-printed one?"

Zahid nodded. "Put a printed oil on canvas next to a hand-created oil, and you'll see the difference immediately. It's unmistakable. If you're sure your forgery is not a printed digital copy, you've got a nearly-impossible task to complete. The kind of forger we're talking about here will be an expert artist in their own right, and might even exhibit and sell their own work." Zahid grinned. "But such artists have a streak of vanity, too. Even though they may have created an unauthorised copy of a work – and that is how they justify creating that forgery to themselves – they often can't help but leave some tell-tale detail that shows that it is their work."

"What sort of detail?" Didier asked.

"It could be anything," said Zahid. "A particular pigment mixture which can only be identified by specialist technical analysis – and that will cost you. It could be something added deep in the background or slightly changed that only an expert will notice. Again, if you want to consult a specialist, it will attract a cost, Jacques. It could be a mark of some sort anywhere within the picture, on the frame, on the stretcher or on any labels on the reverse of the frame. And that's something else you need to understand, Jacques. It's not just the genuine artwork that has to be copied; it's often the frame as well, especially if the forgery is to be sold. The forgery will have to be able to meet fully all the already-existing provenance and any digital records for the work."

Jacques frowned. "But there is no existing provenance for the painting we're looking for, as it has always been in private ownership."

Zahid grinned. "All the more reason to steal the original, replace it with a forgery and then sell it on the open market a few years later. The fact that it has been in private ownership will make it much more desirable to collectors. And a desirable painting from a known artist—"

"Commands a better price." Jacques finished his friend's sentence for him.

"Jacques, have you been able to pinpoint when the exchange might have taken place?"

"Not yet. The forgery was first identified last month, when the painting was returned to the owner. But as it had been on loan for six months, it could have happened at any time during that period." Jacques stared at the whiteboard, possibilities circling in his mind. "It could have happened earlier, too." He turned to Didier. "When we're finished here, I think there are some more avenues we need to explore." He quickly jotted down a couple of notes.

"But what about the original?" Didier asked.

"It's probably already with the new owner, who will be a collector," Zahid replied. "They may be a genuine collector of art who has paid for the item in good faith. But they could also be the commissioner of the crime. Art theft on demand is still a major part of my work, Didier, and I expect it to continue. From what you've told me, I expect that in three, maybe five years' time, that painting will come up for auction. It's unlikely to go on sale here in France, but it will probably turn up somewhere in the Americas or the East. It will be in a country where not too many questions are asked, and through a second- or third-level auction house."

"What do you mean by that?" asked Maxim.

"It won't be one of the prestigious houses like Bonhams, ArtCurial or Christie's, or any other well-known and highly-reputable establishments."

Jacques watched as Zahid's gaze slid from one part of his screen to another. "Any other questions?"

"Just one from me," said Jacques. "Finding the forger, Zahid, what are the chances of that?"

"Very slim, Jacques. The case I've just concluded has been nearly ten years of work. You need the trail of evidence, which requires time, effort and a lot of research, and you need to make sure you follow up every possible lead for as long as it takes."

Jacques baulked at the thought that a criminal could take ten years to track down. Then he reminded himself how long it took to bring Richard Laurent Delacroix to book. *And even now, I still don't really know that man's true identity.*

"OK, Thanks Zahid. Didier, Maxim, any questions?"

They both shook their heads.

"I have one question," said Zahid. "Who's the artist? And I'm not trying to interfere in your case, Jacques. But I might already have some intel that could be useful to you."

Jacques stared at the whiteboard and frowned. "Charles-Marcel Vallade," he said after a considered pause.

"Vallade. Yes, he was often referred to as an Impressionist, but he only followed that artistic style. His work is now recovering from a slump, Jacques. A work previously held in a private collection, coming up for sale now, could currently fetch a minimum of half a million euros. Very likely, two or three times that. Ten, fifteen years ago, nobody would have been that interested. If I come across anything that might help, I'll let you know if I can."

"Thanks, Zahid."

Maxim terminated the video call and then checked his phone. "I've got everything on audio, Jacques," he said. "I'll tidy it up and add it to the shared drive. If you need to re-check anything, you can just pull up the file and fast forward to what you want to hear again."

"Thanks, Maxim."

"It's almost lunchtime," said Jacques. "And I'm not collecting Lucien today as he's eating with his friends in the school dining room. Unless you've other plans, Didier, I thought it might be useful for us to discuss where we go from here with Madame Fribourg's painting over lunch."

"I never turn down invitations like that, Jacques. *Le Drap d'Or* in half an hour?"

Jacques nodded. The short period of time alone would give him an opportunity to marshal his thoughts.

thursday, june 6th, 12.14

Le Drap d'Or, one of the best restaurants in the city, was located to one side of place Urbain V. In the sunshine, diners at the external tables had views of the basilica and Mont Mimat as it towered over the town.

"That call was unexpected," said Jacques as he slipped his phone back into his jacket pocket. "And although I've accepted the commission, I'm not sure what to make of it." He picked up his glass of Sauvignon and took a sip. "Someone has been stealing wood from a farm coppice on the other side of the city."

"Pinching a few logs from someone's wood store? The farmer should know better and keep his fuel in a barn or outhouse he can lock if necessary," said Didier.

"This sounds more industrially managed than that, Didier. The timber was cut from living trees, and others were felled."

Didier frowned and opened his mouth to say something, but stopped. He tasted the Sauvignon and swallowed it back slowly.

"That's different," he said eventually. "And I don't understand why anyone would go to the trouble of stealing wood from living trees. Why not just take the ready-cut stuff from the first available wood shed?"

"I'm puzzled about that myself. But if you can get a load of free timber with just a couple of hours' work, why wouldn't you do that?"

"But selling it on isn't easy, Jacques. You have to declare the source."

"Maybe, but why would you sell it on legitimately? It's more likely that the thief will sell on the black market."

"Any ideas on the possible revenue that could be raised?"

Jacques shook his head. "Until just now, I've never considered illegally felling trees as a prospect for any of our local criminals."

The waiter arrived with the *entrées* and placed two plates of ham on the table, returning a moment later with a basket of bread and some butter.

"Let me have the details, and I'll call out and see whoever it is before I come into the office tomorrow," said Didier. "I expect all we can do is a full security check, provide advice and leave it up to the farmer. Having got the wood, I doubt they will be back."

"We probably need to alert the police, though, Didier. There are plenty of villages up in the forest, and some of the inhabitants will have tracts of forested land that they own, and it will be a source for firewood and various things around their farms."

Didier nodded and spread a thick chunk of butter onto a slice of his *pain*.

"The Vallade," said Jacques after he had demolished his ham and *cornichons*. "I think we need to examine it more closely."

Didier dabbed his serviette at the side of his mouth. "I agree, and I think we should take a look at Madame's photographs. If they are as old as she seemed to suggest, they may not have the fine detail we could get today with a modern digital camera."

"Agreed," said Jacques. "Can you give her a call and ask her to examine the artwork she now has, and get back to us?" He finished his wine.

"Yes. You mentioned in the discussion with Zahid that you thought the picture may have been exchanged at an earlier point."

Jacques nodded. "If Madame only scrutinises the painting when it is returned to her, then there is no reason why it could not have been exchanged when it was still in her possession."

"That would be the period between May and *Toussaint* last year."

Jacques nodded. "If she did her usual checks when it was first returned and she was satisfied then that it was her artwork, she would relax. But that doesn't stop someone from gaining access to the gallery and exchanging it before it has to be packaged and sent to the family later that year."

"We need to—"

Didier paused as the waiter delivered their steak and *frites* and a half-bottle of red wine.

"Yes," said Jacques. "Can you check with Madame for anything suspicious between May and November last year? Any break-in attempts, any alarm system alerts that might have appeared to be false? The information from the *police municipale* about reports of suspicious behaviour in and around the streets surrounding the building. Have we got that yet?"

Didier shook his head.

"Get back onto them. That information is now much more important than I first thought."

Jacques sliced into his medium steak and ate. He glanced around at the nearby tables. They were still empty, but he decided to move the conversation on.

"The security check yesterday morning over in Badaroux. How did that go?"

"Fine," said Didier stabbing his fork into a pile of *frites*. "We should get a commission from the security company handling the installation. The lady seemed very keen to take my advice. I've left her my card so she can call if there are any problems."

"Was that really necessary?"

"I think so, Jacques. She's recently widowed, and her son and his family are now living overseas because of his work. She lives right on the edge of the village, and her nearest neighbouring property is a holiday chalet. I just thought it was appropriate."

Jacques nodded as he swept up the last remnants of his *sauce au poivre* with a forkful of chips, then placed his knife and fork on the plate. "I agree," he said. "If it helps her to feel safer…" He just let the sentence hang unfinished and took a sip from his glass of Merlot.

"Going back to Madame and her painting," said Didier as he dropped his napkin at the side of his plate. "I know Maxim has tracing the Vallade family tree for surviving relatives on his to-do list, but I think we need to know who they are and where they are sooner rather than later. And I think we need to get full details of who is involved with the Trust – whatever that is."

"I agree," said Jacques. "They might be behind the exchange. But it's quite strange to go to such lengths to get something that you believe to be yours, even though there has been a judgement stipulating that ownership rests with someone else."

Didier frowned. "I was thinking the same. If you can afford a fancy lawyer, why not do so again?"

"I want to talk to the carrier this afternoon," said Jacques. "We need to know if it's the same employees who collect and deliver the artwork. If it is the same people every time and the item has been safe until recently, it could be that a new employee might be the weak link. It might be how the exchange was able to take place."

The waiter appeared and cleared the plates. A few moments later, he returned and reeled off a choice of four desserts or cheese. Jacques chose the cheese and Didier the *Iles Flottantes*. They both remained silent until the waiter returned with their orders and left again.

"I think we should also ask for a set of plans for the gallery," Jacques said, as he sliced into a piece of *Pélardon*. "It's an old building. Such places hold secrets. Secrets that, perhaps, not even Madame has any idea about. A set of plans might shed some light on how the original painting could have been exchanged if that happened whilst the original was still in Madame Fribourg's possession." He tore a piece of *pain* in two.

"OK, I'll ask Maxim to get those for us."

The remnants of the meal were consumed in silence. When coffee was offered they both accepted, but the conversation remained halted.

thursday, june 6th, 14.28

Jacques added the new commission he'd received over the phone just after he had reached the restaurant to the list on the whiteboard. He included notes that the case was assigned to Didier and that the following action would be a visit. He made a mental note to update Maxim. As the thought crystallised in his mind, Maxim tapped on the door and walked in.

"I've made some progress on the family of Madame Fribourg," he said.

"Come in and sit down," said Jacques indicating the chair on the other side of his desk.

"I've checked her ID with all her social media and the records. She is who she says she is. Born in Marseille in April 1950, she was the daughter of Madame Alexandrine Chapron. The actual place of birth was in the ninth *arrondissement*. According to her birth record, she was born in the *faubourg* of Mazargues. I've found a marriage for Madame Fribourg, confirming that her maiden name was Chapron."

Jacques pulled his laptop closer, logged on and typed in *Mazargues*. "That's on the eastern side of the city heading out towards the coast," he said, as he looked at the map on the screen. "And Vallade has a connection to Marseille and a ninth district. Although I'm not sure yet if the ninth referred to in the catalogue is in Marseille, Lyon or Toulouse. But I know there is no *faubourg* called Mazargues in Paris."

"I'll check the other cities, shall I?"

"Yes, please. What else have you got?"

"I've checked the old voters' lists for the area, and there is a Madame Chapron, but I can't find a marriage for her or a husband listed at her address."

"Suggesting there may be a question about who her father is," said Jacques.

Maxim nodded. "I've tried to go back further but can't find anything that fits, so I'm still following that through. If Alexandrine Chapron was born elsewhere in France, finding her and her parents might take me a while."

Jacques scowled. "OK," he said. "Keep searching. Madame Fribourg insists that the painting was given to her grandmother. Perhaps we can trace her through the bequests in the will. Where are you with that?"

"I'm still waiting for a copy of the will to arrive. I've been promised that it will be here tomorrow."

"I've updated Vallade's information on the board," said Jacques as he flipped back through the pages of the art book. "But I came across some more personal information about him." Locating the paragraphs he wanted, he speed-read the information. "In 1923, Vallade married an American called Charlotte Adella Rusholme-Knight." Jacques looked up. "I expect she will be quite easy to find, and there is also a son, born two years after the marriage. But there's no name for the child mentioned here."

Maxim reached for the book and jotted down the details. "I'll keep looking," he said.

"One other thing," said Jacques as he stared at his latest addition to the whiteboard. "We have another case, and I've added it to our list. But I was wondering if you could also do some research about the theft of green wood. It's a highly-destructive practice as whole trees are felled, but only as much of the tree's body is cut away as needed. The rest is left on the ground. The client states that he has lost two ancient oaks as a result. He also said that two pines had been felled, and a large chestnut, which was not cut down, has been sliced into and a considerable section of the trunk is now missing. He thinks it is likely he will lose that tree as well. Neither Didier nor I can come up with any reason for such criminal damage. Anything you can find, Maxim, before Didier visits tomorrow morning will be helpful."

Maxim's eyes had widened as he listened to Jacques. "Phew! That's a new one," he said. "I'll try an internet trawl and see what it brings up."

"Thanks, Maxim, but our primary concern is Madame Fribourg and the painting. And has Didier spoken to you about getting a set of plans for the gallery?"

"Yes. I've spoken to the building owner, and he will drop off a set of blueprints sometime tomorrow."

"Thanks, Maxim."

Jacques pulled out the business card that Madame Fribourg had given him the previous afternoon. The number quoted was a landline, and there was a website. Jacques turned to his laptop and typed in the web address.

The couriers, Labalte et Baptiste, had a modern website that was easy to navigate. Jacques went straight to the *About Us* section. The company was set up by two brothers in 1926. It was now managed by a grandson of one of the original owners and his business partner. The business was located in Quimper, but handled packages of all sizes throughout the country. They also handled removals, including taking on the packing of all items in readiness for a move, and offered storage space for furniture for short- and long-term leases. Jacques quickly checked through some of the testimonials. Everything online seemed to indicate that the company was well respected. Jacques phoned the number on the card and got through to a young lady.

"Madame, I'm making some enquiries about the movement of an artwork from here in Mende to Finistère… Yes, it's from the gallery on rue du Soubeyran, Mende…" He waited as she checked for the details. When she came back on the line, she referred him to Monsieur Georges Nolin, who had a small secure industrial unit on the outskirts of the city, explaining that they used trusted local contractors.

thursday, june 6th, 15.48

Nolin's industrial unit carried the signage of Labalte et Baptiste. Monsieur Nolin was dressed in the corporate uniform of the removal company. The introductory pleasantries dispensed with, Jacques got straight to the point.

"Monsieur Nolin, thanks for seeing me at such short notice. I understand that you recently delivered an artwork to the gallery on rue du Soubeyran on the first of last month."

"Yes, I did."

"And did you collect the artwork from Finistère?"

"No, that's not how this works," he said. "Single packages, even ones that must be kept securely, go through our transport network. That package would have gone first to our central depot in Quimper. From there, it would have been transported, along with many other single packages, to Tours, where we have another depot. From Tours, it came to me here, and I delivered it to the gallery on the first."

"At the depots in Quimper and Tours, how is the handover from the depot to the driver managed?"

"Everything is signed in and signed out. When the driver arrived with the package, I had to sign his manifest to say that I had received the item. I then had to check it in on the computer system. When I was ready to drive into Mende with everything I had to deliver that day, I checked the item out on the system and delivered it. Madame Fribourg had to sign my manifest to show that she had taken delivery of the package. I updated the system remotely. Everything is recorded, Monsieur Forêt."

Jacques tapped his pen against his notebook as he thought about his next question.

"Is your company responsible for packaging secure items like works of art, for example?"

"Yes, and we have specialist staff who work with museum conservators to do that."

"So, are you aware of any of the content of the packages that you deliver?"

"Not as such, no. But I've been delivering that package to the gallery for the last ten years, and it's not difficult to guess that what's in there is a work of art."

"Is your computer system able to track the location of an item at any point on its journey?"

"Yes, of course. We have to be able to provide absolute assurance for our customers that their valuable items are secure whilst in transit."

"Thanks, Monsieur Nolin. I think I've got everything I need."

Jacques left the small office and sauntered back to his car. "If the painting is tracked from the moment it leaves the Trust in Finistère," he said as he put the key in the ignition, "then it could have been exchanged whilst it was there." He turned the key and set the engine running.

Back in his office, Jacques dumped his car keys on the desk and walked through to the main office.

"My visit to the couriers has got us no further," he said as he perched on the corner of Didier's desk. "They track everything with a state-of-the-art computer system."

"Makes sense when you consider the potential sale value of the items they might be moving."

"If the real artwork was exchanged for the forgery, it must have happened either at the Trust or at Madame Fribourg's little gallery."

Didier frowned. "Of the two, I'd say it's more likely to be the gallery."

"But how did they do it, Didier? The picture isn't small. Anyone walking out with it would be noticed. Taking the canvas out of the frame and replacing it with another one takes time and requires expert knowledge. How did they do it?"

Didier shrugged.

friday, june 7th, 08.18

The traffic heading south out of Mende at seven-thirty that morning had been heavier than Didier had remembered or guessed it would be. Once he hit the narrow lanes that would take him to his destination, the other cars were sparse, but the progress was almost equally slow because of the twists and turns. The single-track road was overshadowed by trees, the surface rough, and there was evidence of small landslides from last winter's snow. Didier took his time as he headed along to *Ferme* Sallan.

The farmhouse wall rose straight out of the side of the road on his right. Didier slowed to a snail's pace as he looked for the entrance to the yard. Turning in, a few metres further along the road, he found *Fermier* Sallan waiting for him in a tractor with the engine running.

"Monsieur Forêt," he said, jumping down and holding out his hand. "*Bonjour.* Thanks for coming out all this way."

Didier shook his hand. "I'm Didier Duclos," he said. "My colleague is engaged on another case at the moment, but he told me about your call yesterday."

Fermier Sallan sniffed.

"I've come in place of Jacques because we wanted to follow up on the..." *Should I call it theft?* "...on the damage done to the trees as quickly as we could." Didier waited to see if the farmer's expression would change from complete disdain to something more welcoming. But it didn't. The man just jumped up onto his tractor.

"The copse is a kilometre away across the field. Stand on the running board and hold on here." He pointed to a grab-handle that was as grubby as the farmer's blue overalls.

"It's not damage," he said as he shifted the tractor into gear and set off with a lurch. "It's little better than vandalism, what they've done to my trees," he shouted above the machine's noise. "Blatant vandalism. That's what it is. Some of those trees were more than two hundred years old." The tractor took a nosedive as the farmer turned it onto a sloping terrain and set off across the lush pale green land towards a long stand of trees at the bottom of the field.

"I've had to put the cattle in the next pasture," he said. The tone of the bald statement was such that Didier took the comment to mean that his presence might have upset the animals.

Finally coming to a stop, Didier stepped down. He'd been gripping the handle so tightly he'd almost lost the circulation in his hands. He stretched and relaxed his fingers to try and get some feeling back.

"It's through here," said *Fermier* Sallan as he walked with a rolling gait around to one side of the copse and opened a five-bar gate that had seen some years. "There's no straight path through. It's all rough ground, so watch your step," he cautioned as he started working his way through the undergrowth between the trees.

A few metres in, Didier saw the first evidence of the damage. What had once been a tall pine lay flat on the ground, its canopy still intact but the bottom section of the trunk wholly removed. The wood chips from the felling and the cutting were strewn on either side of where the tree lay.

"That's about two metres of timber they've had there."

Didier pulled out his phone and took detailed photos of the scene. He also captured the stump of the trunk. "It's a clean cut," he said.

"*Oui*." The farmer spat out the word with such force Didier froze momentarily.

"That's a logging man," he said. The venom in his tone was undisguised. "Whoever has done this is a logging man. Only an experienced logger can cut that cleanly."

Didier nodded. "And the other trees?"

"There's four more." The farmer set off further into the heart of the small wood. "There's one more pine through there," he said, pointing to his left. "If you want to look.

What you've not seen yet is even worse. This way."

Didier watched as the farmer ducked below the low branches of a tree and disappeared. Stepping carefully, he followed and emerged into a small glade. A large sprawling chestnut tree stood in the centre, covered by dappled sunlight.

"Fine tree that." The farmer stood and looked it up and down. "It's other side you need to see."

Didier followed the man around the base of the tree. The trunk had been cut through to the centre at the bottom, and again just below the canopy. In the space between was nothing but the exposed heart of the tree. The surrounding ground was strewn with sawdust and small wood chips.

Didier was aghast. "Will the tree survive this level of damage?"

Fermier Sallan sniffed and moved closer to the open wound on the trunk. He placed his hand on it as though he were checking for a heartbeat. "It's healthy enough. There's no disease, but they've cut right through to the heart. Look." He pointed at the tree rings. "It might survive, but I've got to think about any further damage that might be caused if we get one of our north-westerlies this autumn. That canopy is a lot of weight, and this tree has lost half its base. Won't take much to blow it over, which will damage other trees."

Didier stopped taking photographs for a moment. "So you'll have to fell the rest of it then?"

The farmer nodded. "*Oui.*" Again the spat-out affirmation.

I must be asking the wrong questions. Didier kept the thought to himself. "But if it's good wood, you'll be able to sell some of the resulting timber, won't you?"

The farmer stuffed his hands into the pockets of his overalls. "That's the thing, you see. That tree is almost three hundred years old. Do you know the paperwork involved in felling it, even though it's on my land, and then selling the wood on?"

Suitably admonished, Didier looked away and moved around the tree to take some more photographs.

"There are two very old oaks just as bad. Do you want to see them as well?"

Didier shook his head. "A few questions if I may?"

"Go on."

"You say this is the work of a logger. That means whoever did it brought a chainsaw or some other tool—"

"Chainsaw."

"Right. The farmhouse is only a kilometre away. Did no one hear anything?"

"No. Nothing. Between here and the farmhouse is an old stone barn and my woodshed. We heard nothing."

"When did you last cut any wood here?"

"A while ago. Me and my brother hadn't planned on cutting any wood until later in the year. But that's changed now."

"So, if no one heard anything and you had no reason to be here, it's not possible to see the damage from the field or the road. What drew your attention to the problem?"

"The cattle. Whoever came the night before last and did this left the gate open. First thing yesterday morning, a couple of my cattle were paying too much attention to the entrance to the wood. I checked it out. Then I phoned my brother. He jointly owns the wood with me. He's got a farm of his own seven kilometres away on the far side of the next village. He came over and we decided we needed to talk to someone. I talked to your boss, and my brother talked to the police."

Didier waited for him to say more. "And the police have advised?"

"They haven't even been out to see the damage."

"OK. Did they say when they would be able to take a look?"

The farmer shook his head. "It'll be like the time my brother's log store got broken into. Nobody came for a week, and then we never heard no more." *Fermier* Sallan stomped back through the trees and out towards the edge of the wood. Didier followed quickly behind. He wasn't sure he could find his way on his own.

"I'm off for my bite of something to eat. You're welcome to stay and join me if you've got more questions."

"Thanks," said Didier as he stepped on the running board. "A coffee will be fine."

The farmhouse kitchen was untidy and old, and well-used. *How can anyone live with all this clutter?* Didier's gaze drifted from the sink and draining board with half-washed pots, to the large dresser along one wall full of cups, plates and dishes of various patterns, to the heavy wooden table with the farmer sitting at one end noisily chomping into toasted bread surrounding substantial portions of cheese and ham.

"Will they come back?" Madame Sallan asked, as she put a wide-rimmed cup of coffee on the table for Didier.

"I think it's unlikely," said Didier. "There are plenty of other isolated farms all around this area and I'm sure they won't want to risk walking into a trap by returning here. But that shouldn't stop you from improving security for your own peace of mind."

"What are you suggesting?" *Fermier* Sallan put his large chunk of a sandwich on his plate.

"I'm not suggesting anything," said Didier. "But you might want to make the gate to the copse more secure with a heavy padlock and chain. The wood is bound on two sides by a wall. You might want to raise the height of that. And on the other two sides, you might want to think about higher, more secure fencing."

"So, you're not going to go out and look for these men then?"

"I'm sorry, but we haven't the workforce, *Fermier* Sallan. We're a small organisation and we can advise you on security, and if you want the expense we can suggest where to install some surveillance cameras to make your property safer. But," Didier shook his head. "In truth, Monsieur, just fixing those walls and the fences and ensuring the gate locks securely is probably the best you can do. As I said, these people are not likely to come back."

"And what about my stolen timber? Five trees, that's over five hundred euros if it were for sale. What are you going to do about getting that back?"

Only five hundred euros? Didier thought back to the detailed email he'd received from Maxim just after he had got home. *More like a thousand euros.* Until he had read Maxim's message, Didier had had no idea that there was a market for good quality green wood, not only in France but internationally. He'd been astounded at the extent of the problem in North America, and the photographs of the damage done to significant areas of the redwood forests. The damage inflicted on the American continent may be massive in comparison with the issue *Fermier* Sallan was facing, but in Didier's book theft was still theft.

"I'll alert the *Garde Forestier* to look out for similar incidents, and the police and the local *mairie* to look for rogue traders at markets, local fêtes and events. Before I took up this work, I was a policeman, Monsieur, so I will also telephone an ex-colleague in Mende and ask him to trawl the internet for under-the-counter timber sales."

Fermier Sallan sniffed and nodded. "And I suppose on top of my other losses, I've got to fork out some fee or other because you've come here."

Didier looked at the depressing state of the kitchen. *Not decorated for at least thirty years.*

"No," he said. "There's no charge for this visit." He looked *Fermier* Sallan directly in the eye and waited for his response.

"That's fair enough," his wife said. "That's fair, isn't it, Gérard?"

"I suppose so," he grumbled as he got to his feet. "I'll show you out then."

Didier nodded to Madame Sallan and followed his client outside.

"Watch how you go on the lane," he said. "My neighbour will be bringing his beasts down soon."

Didier smiled. "Thanks, and..." He wanted to offer further assistance if it might be needed in the future, but decided against it. *It will be grudgingly accepted.* He got in his car and put his keys in the ignition. As he drove off the property, the farmer raised his hand.

"Was that in thanks or in relief?" Didier asked himself as he glanced in the rear-view mirror before turning into the narrow road. *Most probably deep distrust.* And the thought settled in his mind as he carefully picked his way back to the main road north to Mende.

mazargues in the 9th, friday, may 10th, 08.47

The cool of the morning was a refreshing change from the previous day as Madame Roşu hurried along boulevard des Anges to her employer's house. Passing the studio, she glanced left to see if anything had changed. When she left on Wednesday morning, all the blinds were open. It was her job to leave the blinds open unless she had been left a note not to do so. Madame Roşu was pleased to see that the blinds were open this morning, which meant that her employer had already started work in the studio. She trusted that her money for Wednesday would be with her money for today, so Madame Roşu quickened her step.

A few houses further along, the cleaner reached the dead-end of the street. The property on the right was her destination. She opened the wrought-iron gate and detached a flapping striped piece of plastic tape that had been tied in place. The reason for its presence and how it got there was of no concern to her.

She stopped as she moved past the postbox to the immediate left of the gate. There was some post that had got trapped in the letterbox.

"The postman is very early today." As she closed the gate behind her and walked the short path to the front door, she wondered why her employer hadn't emptied the postbox before leaving for the studio.

She slotted her key into the lock and dismissed the oddity of the postbox with the newly-realised conclusion that the postman must have visited between her employer leaving and her own arrival. She frowned when she considered that even that possibility was unusual.

"Must be a new postman," she said. Madame Roşu set her basket down on the floor in the small vestibule. She removed her jacket, neatly folded it and placed it over the handle of the pannier. The house was silent and tidy as always, but the usual lingering aroma of fresh coffee was missing.

Feeling in her overall pocket, she took out the slip of paper that her daughter had written out for her. But, having seen the open blinds at the studio, she felt sure there would be no problems today. And if there were, she would just slip into the studio on her way home and address her questions to the painter in person.

Madame Roşu had a system for getting all her jobs done. It was always the bedroom first, the *salon* and the vestibule next, then the bathroom, and the kitchen last. The house was small, all on one level, nicely proportioned, and very comfortably decorated. Sorina looked up at the light in the centre of the vestibule and sniffed. Not all of the decoration was to Madame Roşu's taste, but she recognised quality when she saw it. The artist's house was the kind of small property she had once wished for herself in retirement. But her husband had died whilst all four of her children were still at school, and she'd had to work, scrimp and save to keep the family together.

"Perhaps one day," she sighed as she collected all the cleaning materials and equipment from the cupboard in the kitchen and went through to the bedroom.

As she worked her way through the house, she became increasingly aware that nothing, or perhaps more accurately very little, had been moved or changed since her last visit two weeks ago. Although she was required to clean the studio every Wednesday morning, she was only needed at the house on alternate Fridays.

In the bedroom, only two bottles of perfume were set out on the dressing table. She put them away in the drawer, but thought it was odd that there weren't the usual four or five as there had been on her last visit and most of her visits before that.

In the bathroom, the shower was completely dry as though it had not been used that morning, and when she tidied the towels, she found no dampness on them at all.

"Perhaps Madame was up very early today." As she moved onto the *salon*, that thought got caught up with the early delivery of the post, and her mind started to whirl in a very distracting spiral.

"Sorina, get on with your work and stop imagining things," she told herself. In the *salon*, the magazines on the coffee table had barely been touched. Madame Roşu just tidied and dusted and polished.

But it was what she found in the kitchen that provided that final convincing evidence that something was quite definitely amiss. She stared down at the empty sink. The beautifully hand-painted breakfast coffee cup, saucer, and matching plate she expected to see waiting to be washed up were not there. She looked over at the worktop. The *cafetière* was in its usual place. It had not been used that morning either. Just to be certain that she had not missed anything, the cleaner opened the cupboard above where the *cafetière* stood. The crockery she expected to find in the sink was stacked on the lowest shelf. When she turned and looked at the far right corner of the window sill, the small cactus in the pale grey earthenware pot sat alone. Usually, her envelope containing the money for Friday's work was propped up against it. But not today.

Madame Roşu finished all her remaining tasks as quickly as possible. And instead of leaving a note, she determined to go and see her employer in person at the studio on her way back to the apartment.

Her jacket on, her basket over her arm, she locked up and strode down the street with a purpose.

mende, friday, june 7th, 10.04

"I've finally got the details of the exhibition in New York in 1929, Jacques." Didier breezed into the office. "And we've got more than we asked for, or more than I thought we would get in response."

"Good," said Jacques. Didier marched over to the sofa, sat down and placed some sheets of paper on the table. A couple had entries starred with a bright pink marker pen.

"There were three of Vallade's paintings submitted to the exhibition." He looked down at the first relevant page and read the details. "'Portrait in Black and White, Côte d'Opale', and our painting. Those last two were shown in one room together."

"'Portrait in Black and White' is mentioned in one of the chapters I read the other day." Jacques jumped up, got the book, and began flicking through the pages. "Yes. Here. P03, and it's in Chapter Four… This painting was completed during his travels in Italy," said Jacques as he opened the book on the right page.

Didier grinned. "We have a digitised copy of the exhibition catalogue. The archivist scanned all the pages and emailed them. It's a substantial document, and I've only printed the pages that are relevant to our enquiry. But the details in the listings are interesting, Jacques."

Didier pulled out three other pages from underneath the first set. "The most interesting details are about our picture," he said, pushing the sheet towards his colleague.

"But that's not our painting," said Jacques. "The perspective isn't right. That shoreline is at a less acute angle than in our picture." Jacques got up and took the copy of the image from under the magnets on the whiteboard. Sitting down again, he placed the printed image against the one in the New York exhibition catalogue. He looked from one version of the painting to the other and back again.

"There are colour differences, too." Jacques looked up and stared at Didier. "Have you any idea what this might mean?"

"I think it can only mean one thing," said Didier. "There must be more than one copy – no, more than one version of the same scene."

"Or the canvas sent to New York was also a forgery."

"Perhaps. But I wouldn't expect a reputable organisation like a world-renowned museum in New York to be duped. Would you?"

Jacques got up and moved to the window. "This case is getting more and more frustrating by the hour."

"I asked for details of who submitted the paintings and who actually agreed to the loan, as it seemed possible they may not be the same person in each case. The museum has included scanned images of their old ledgers."

Didier placed a copy of an entry in front of Jacques. "According to this ledger, Vallade himself agreed to the loan of all three works, but they were all delivered to the museum from three different addresses." Didier pointed to one of the columns on the far right of the page. "The portrait was shipped from Italy—"

"That makes sense," said Jacques. "That is the portrait of Vicontessa Lucrezia Santini. He met her while travelling in Italy, and it was known that she modelled for him and that their relationship later became more intimate."

"The second one, 'Côte d'Opale', was shipped from Finistère, but the third one, 'Sunday Afternoon on the Beach', was shipped from Pas de Calais. Look at the city name for the sender's address, Boulogne-sur-Mer."

Jacques grimaced. "Thanks, Didier, that just makes our search significantly more complicated." Jacques let out a deep sigh. "I think I might have to call back into the library and get the other three volumes of the catalogue. I'm also speaking to Madame Rouvière, the daughter of the catalogue author, this afternoon. I will ask for her views on the possibility of more than one copy of the work."

Didier nodded. "The visit this morning to *Ferme* Sallan was... different," he said, finally satisfied with his choice of description.

Jacques grinned. "Let me guess. A difficult and demanding *fermier*?"

"Bluff, I think, is a word I would also use." Didier pulled out his phone and scrolled through the gallery to the first of the photos of the damaged trees. "I had a lot of sympathy for him, Jacques. When you see the extent of the damage, and understand that the trees are hundreds of years old and will not recover, and will have to be felled because of the wanton vandalism, it's heartbreaking. I've never considered myself a tree-hugger, but after this morning..." Didier shook his head.

Jacques looked up. "This is monstrous. How do you suggest we take this forward?"

Didier shrugged. "I don't know. I thought about installing CCTV, but the copse is at the bottom of a field a kilometre from the house. There's no electricity supply other than a mobile battery attached to a solar panel linked to his electric fencing for the cattle. So, I can't see how that can help. The other thing that occurred to me whilst there was that the people who took the wood are not likely to return. I didn't think installing surveillance cameras would be a worthwhile expense for the farmer."

"No, you're probably right."

"The wood was surrounded by a wall on two sides and the usual stake-and-wire fences you see all over the area. The walls were in disrepair, and there was no lock on the old wooden gate at the entrance to the wood."

"Just like most of the other farms."

Didier nodded. "He didn't need a security expert to tell him that, so I waived the fee. I know we need every penny we can get at the moment, Jacques, but I couldn't charge him. I only saw the kitchen, but the inside of the house looked as desperate and as dilapidated as the outside."

"No, that's fine, Didier." Jacques held up the picture of

the large chestnut. "Will that need to be cut down?"

"Yes. *Fermier* Sallan said that it could easily become unstable in a high north-westerly and cause further damage to nearby trees."

"And the value of the timber lost?"

"The farmer said he thought it would be around five hundred euros. I think it might be more. I was looking at the price of oak, pine and chestnut last night once I'd got Maxim's email. The true value could be a lot more than his estimate."

"And I suppose there were no footprints or tyre tracks."

"It's been too dry recently, and the theft was the night before last. The local police have been informed but have not yet investigated."

"And the *Garde Forestier*, are they aware there is a problem in the area?"

"Yes. I've already spoken to them. This incident isn't the first. There are two farms near Mont Mimat and a couple more outlying properties north of Mende. There has been some incursion on forestry land, too. They've noted the details, and their advice is to stay vigilant and report anything unusual."

"Do we have any idea why this is happening?"

"It's like all forms of crime, Jacques. If you can get around the rules and get something for free and then sell it on, why not?"

"But this isn't just about getting goods for free, Didier. There's an ecological aspect too."

"I know, and that makes it all the more sinister. Especially when you consider that the people taking the wood are probably experienced loggers."

"How sure are you the perpetrators are loggers?"

"I'm not sure, but *Fermier* Sallan was certain. He said the cutting was too neat and too well-executed."

"Get back on to the police, Didier. Knowing these men work or have worked in the logging industry is a starting point for a full-time investigation. The police and the *Garde Forestier* are the only organisations that can cover enough ground to catch these people. Make sure they see these photos, and, if necessary, get our client into the station to make a formal statement."

"OK. One last thing, Jacques. The Sforza investigation. I don't like the apparent complete absence of information about him prior to five years ago. I want to go down to Marseille and check out the properties he owns in the northern quarter of the city, and his property outside the city too. Alain is also meeting Sforza on his yacht over the weekend. I thought I might stake it out and get some photos of him. We can do a look-up from that. It might be interesting to see who else he associates with."

"That's fine. Just keep the expenses to the minimum, please."

"I also have some business of my own down there, so I'm happy to foot the bill, Jacques."

"OK, thanks."

"I'll be leaving about twelve, if that's OK with you?"

"Yes, that's fine, and thanks, Didier. Enjoy your weekend."

mazargues in the 9th, friday, may 10th, 11.52

Out of breath and with beads of sweat on her brow, Madame Roşu stood outside the building that housed her employer's studio. A few moments later, she was pressing the buzzer for Unit B1. But the front door did not click open. She tried again, and when there was still no response, she keyed in the code and went inside.

Hurrying up the stairs, she paused outside the studio door, tapped lightly and waited.

"Madame Apollinaire, *c'est moi*," she shouted in her heavily accented French whilst knocking as hard as she could.

"Madame Apollinaire?" After a few moments of deliberation, she fished out her bunch of keys and let herself in. Rushing into the centre of the space, she came to an abrupt halt. No one was there. The door to the kitchen area was wide open just as she had left it, and nothing in the studio had been moved or touched since she was last there.

"Perhaps she has gone out to avoid me," muttered Sorina. But that didn't make any sense. Madame Apollinaire had her daughter's phone number, and could have telephoned if there had been a problem.

Madame Roşu moved across to the first easel. She thought that if her employer had been working that morning, then the paint would be wet. Lifting the corner of the grubby white cloth draped across it, she looked at the partially-completed portrait. The whole picture looked dry. Moving across the second easel, she lifted the sheet and found that picture was also dry. She let the sheet drop back into place. Striding across to the kitchen area, a quick look confirmed to the cleaner that no one had been in the studio since she had left on Wednesday.

Madame Roşu stood in the kitchen. The forty-five euros she was due to be paid for this week's work was the only money she had for herself. She knew her daughter would always look after her, but Sorina was accustomed to her little bit of cash. It enabled her to send small presents home to Romania for her eldest son's children, now five, nine and thirteen. With a few euros of her own, she could buy little treats for her daughter or occasionally offer something towards a bill for the apartment she shared with Elena and her son-in-law. Madame Apollinaire's little envelopes of money enabled Sorina to feel a measure of independence and provided the occasional indulgence. A wave of worry spread through her stomach as she wondered if her opportunity to keep her self-esteem had ended.

Stepping back into the studio, Madame Roşu looked around as though it might be her last opportunity to be in or see an artist's workspace. She was suddenly filled with dread as her gaze shifted across the windows.

"If Madame Apollinaire has not been here since Wednesday, then…" Dropping her basket, she rushed to the windows and closed the blinds immediately as her employer's words, translated by her daughter, echoed through her mind: *She needs light to work, but the dark blinds protect the pictures. If she's not coming to the studio on a Wednesday, she will leave a note telling you to leave the blinds closed.*

"Oh no, the pictures," wailed Sorina. As her heart rate began to climb with the certainty that she may have damaged the paintings somehow, Sorina began to sob and pulled out a handkerchief from the pocket of her overalls. With the studio now quite dark and sombre, Madame Roşu collected her things and let herself out.

"I'll ask Elena when she comes home," she said as she wiped her eyes before running down the stairs. Once outside, she strode away, shoulders hunched and head down. She just wanted to get away as quickly as possible.

mende, friday, june 7th, 14.28

Jacques dropped the three remaining volumes of the Vallade catalogue on his desk. He wasn't sure that he needed them for his current investigation, but he wanted to read them anyway, and there was always the possibility that a useful nugget of personal information might be hidden away within the pages.

This latest trip to the library had been irritation-free, and he'd made a mental note to always return immediately after lunch on a Friday afternoon in future. Jacques pulled out his phone, set the alarm for 14.55 and placed it on the desk in front of him. He could not afford to miss the meeting with Madame Rouvière at three. At the same time, he was anxious to look at the book on Vallade's portraiture, particularly the listing for *Portrait in Black and White*.

As was his habit, he scanned the whiteboard for any updates from Maxim and any additional notes that might have been stuck there in his absence.

"Good, we've finally got the will," he said as he logged onto his laptop and navigated through to the file listed on the shared drive. He clicked the document open, and as soon as it formed on the screen, he minimised it. He would look at that after he'd spoken to Madame Rouvière. The second note on the board said FAM TREE VALL with a file listing beneath. Jacques noted the file name and stuck a message to his laptop.

"I'll look at that once Lucien is in bed."

Having caught up, he could not stop himself from checking the index at the back of the second volume of the catalogue, and turned immediately to the appropriate page.

The listing covered almost the whole page on the left, with the one on the right filled with a copy of the canvas.

Jacques gazed at the woman's face. The flesh tone of her skin was almost deathly pale, and the hair a deep chestnut in contrast. Her pose was elegant, with what appeared to be an element of disdain for the viewer or maybe genuine disdain for the painter.

"And, yet they became lovers," said Jacques. The turn of the head gave the viewer a profile as the Vicontessa looked out of the painting to her left. The full-length, figure-hugging dress she was wearing was intended to be worn for an evening event. But the light shining across the picture from the top right of the page to the bottom left suggested it might be late afternoon, or possibly early on a midsummer evening. The black velvet of the gown and the spill of light the inspiration for the title of the picture. *I suppose an art critic would call that pose classical.* Jacques held the book at arm's length. She was undoubtedly a striking young woman, and it was apparent that the painter had represented his subject at her most alluring. *I think he must have known her intimately when this was finished.* The background was plain, and Jacques wondered why.

The alarm on his phone rang, and the book nearly ended up on the floor. He managed to keep sufficient hold to prevent it from tipping backwards and off the edge of his desk. Quickly shoving a spare bit of paper in the page, he set the volume on top of the others, turned his attention to the video call with Madame Rouvière and dialled in. It was a couple of minutes after the hour before she joined him on screen.

"Madame Rouvière, thank you for making time to speak to me today. I'm Jacques Forêt, and I'm undertaking some research in connection with a couple of paintings by Charles-Marcel Vallade. I'm hoping that you might be able to help me."

"You're welcome, Monsieur, but I'm not sure how much I can tell you. My father was the expert on Vallade."

"Yes, Madame, I am aware of that. I've got the four volumes of your father's catalogue of Vallade's work. It's interesting reading," he said. "I notice that your father and

Vallade had a lengthy correspondence, and I was wondering what happened to those letters."

"They are mostly in the archive at the Vallade house in Finistère. When *Papa* died in 2001, my brothers left me to sort out all his papers, research notes and letters. My father had always made it quite clear that when he died, he wanted all his papers to be gifted to the Vallade Museum. It took me almost two years to go through everything, index it, and get everything ordered before I could formally hand over the cache to the Trustees. The archivist is still there, and it's Madame Carolyne Truchon. By all means, contact her. I'm sure Carolyne will be only too pleased to help you."

"Thank you." Jacques jotted down the name. "Putting together the catalogue must have been something of a lifetime's work for your father."

"Yes, it was. And for quite a bit of that time, I helped him. I have three boys, Monsieur, and whilst they were young, and before I went back to full-time work, I was doing whatever I could to support my father."

"The quotes from letters in the book, I'm assuming they —"

"Yes. Some are from letters that my father received from the artist. Others are from family correspondence gifted to the Trust by Vallade himself just before he died. All of that is also part of Carolyne's responsibility."

"Can I ask how your father collected all the details of the various works in the catalogue?"

"It was a very long and slow process. It involved numerous calls in newspapers and art magazines for information about particular works, or more general calls for owners to come forward. It also involved contacting museums and galleries worldwide to give us details of the works they held. And of course, some of the items held by galleries were not actually in situ when we asked for information. We had to wait until those pieces were returned. In one instance it was ten years before we could finalise the listings for..." Her brow furrowed. "Eight, yes, it was eight paintings, plus three watercolours and four sketches. They all belonged to a private collector who had the works out on loan to various establishments across the English-speaking continents."

"And what about 'Sunday Afternoon on the Beach', Madame? Is there anything you can tell me about that?"

Madame Rouvière looked to her left and frowned. "I'm not entirely sure I can recall which picture that is, Monsieur. Just a moment." She disappeared from the screen, and Jacques could hear books being moved and pages flicked backwards and forwards.

"Ah yes. I've got it here. Yes, it's a beautifully serene painting, isn't it?" She held her copy of the catalogue up to the screen. "Yes, I remember sifting through a number of letters between *Papa* and Vallade discussing this work. I can't recall the precise details of those discussions, but Carolyne will be able to help you with that."

"OK. Thank you. What about authorised copies of Vallade's paintings, Madame? Do you know anything about that?"

Madame Rouvière shook her head. "Not that much. I know from the correspondence that Vallade was adamant that his work should not be copied and... What was the word? And cheapened. He thought having copies of his works printed on cards was a debasement of the art itself, and he saw it as a personal insult."

Jacques wondered if all artists were as vain as Vallade. All he could see was a missed opportunity to advertise his skill as a painter and the possibility of a second income-stream from the sale of copies.

"Did he authorise any copies of his work at any time?"

"I think so, yes. But I'm sure it was only two or three oils on canvas in the whole of his lifetime."

"Can you remember which ones?"

"One was a stunning seascape looking out over the Château d'If. He'd painted that whilst he was living in Mazargues. There are several panels of the same scene but with slightly different perspectives. It was a favourite of my father's. When I was going through the papers, I discovered that *Papa* finally persuaded Vallade to allow a limited number of copies to be made. I now have the copy that was gifted to my father by the artist. They occasionally come up for sale and can command quite a good price."

"And the other copied works?"

"I don't know, Monsieur Forêt. Perhaps Carolyne can help you with that. What I do know is that since Vallade's death, the Trust has made other works available for copying, but I've no idea which ones or how many."

"OK. Thank you." Jacques jotted down another note as a reminder for his discussion with the archivist. "Madame, something else that has been puzzling me is the accuracy of the information in your father's books. It took the professor over forty years to compile the content. There must be—"

"I'm sorry?" Madame Rouvière visibly bristled, and her tone hardened to steel. "Monsieur Forêt, my father took great pains to ensure that the content within the catalogue was as accurate as possible at the point of the manuscript going to print. I do not deny that some things will have changed since then. Paintings are coming up for sale since publication, and others being acquired by galleries or museums. That happens all the time. But, no, if you are intimating that my father's work was sloppy, then I can state categorically that you are wrong."

"Madame, please accept my apology. I did not wish to offend. But, in connection with my research, Professor Simmonet states for 'Sunday Afternoon on the Beach'..." Jacques reached across and picked up his copy of Volume One of the catalogue. It was already open at the page he needed. "'There are no auction or exhibition records for the present work'." He looked up. "That's a direct quote from your father's published notes on the painting. If you want to check, you'll find the listing on page one hundred and forty-eight. My research has shown that 'Sunday Afternoon on the Beach' was on display at an exhibition in New York in 1929. The museum ledgers show that Vallade himself agreed to the loan, and that a Madame Guiot, then living in Boulogne-sur-Mer, submitted the work on Vallade's behalf."

Jacques waited for a response.

Madame Rouvière had her volume of the book in front of her, and Jacques could hear the frenzied movement of pages. After a moment, she lifted her head and took a breath.

"You're right. It does say that. I am not able to comment on why that is the case. Perhaps Carolyne can help you better than I."

"Have you ever heard of, or come across anything about, a Madame Guiot in the professor's papers, Madame?"

"Not that I can recall."

"And the name, it means nothing to you?"

"No. Perhaps Carolyne can help."

"There are also notes in the book about works being gifted to individuals or organisations. How accurate would you say those statements might be?"

"I would say they were absolutely accurate at the point the catalogue went to print. If you turn to the back of the final volume, there is a form of disclaimer stating exactly that. I can't be held responsible for what might have happened after the books were published."

Jacques waited, expecting to be referred once again to Carolyne the archivist. Madame Rouvière remained still and silent, her face set like a stone and her lips pursed.

I don't think there's anything more to be explored here.

"OK. Thank you for your time, Madame, and I will follow up my other questions with Carolyne at the museum." He smiled, clicked out of the video link and shoved his laptop to the back of the desk. "And the puzzle just got harder," he said as he stared at the whiteboard.

Within seconds the alarm on his phone pinged again. Jacques jumped up and collected his jacket. It was school time, and hopefully Amélie would be at the school gates and give him the answer he was expecting concerning Alain's offer. He ran down the four flights of stairs and out of the building. It was a ten-minute walk across the city to the school that Lucien attended. As Jacques strode along the pavement, he wagered with himself that he'd make the school entrance in eight minutes and thirty seconds. It was a stupid bet, and there was no monetary gain, but it took the mundanity out of the everyday usualness of the regular Friday school run.

Coming to a halt outside the school, he checked his watch. "Eight minutes forty-five," he said to himself. *I can shave that down more before the end of the school year, and I will.* He waited as more parents and grandparents gathered. He stared across to the central doorway.

"Jacques." Amélie came towards him. "I've thought about Alain's offer, and I know it's generous, but I'm not going to take it. I only took on the *crèche* because it helped me with Jeannette, but she's eight now, and little Isabelle will be six soon, and... When you were... Well, when Lucien joined the *crèche*, I was only too happy to look after them both, but Lucien is going to be seven next month – oh, and he's still talking about wanting a dog for his birthday, Jacques. He's mentioned that just about every day this week."

"I know, and I'm still thinking about it." A pause ensued. "You were telling me about Alain's offer."

"Oh! Yes. Well, now that my two are getting older and Lucien is getting quite independent, I was hoping that I could move away from the Earth Mother role a bit. Perhaps take on more work for the investigations, the budget, or some of the admin so that you can use Maxim more. I'm just looking for anything that is different from childcare and, well, children. I want to do some grown-up stuff for a change, and—"

Jacques didn't catch the last bit of the conversation as Amélie's light voice was drowned out by a mass of excited children rushing out of the school building, eager to get home and play because it was the last day of the week.

"*Papa.*" Lucien skidded to a halt beside his dad. Jacques ruffled his son's hair.

"Did you have a good day today?"

"Yes. And I've got a picture for Monsieur Didier."

"Oh well, we'll look at that when we get back to the

office. Are you carrying your rucksack today?" Jacques held out his hand, expecting Lucien to slip the bag off his shoulders and give it to him as he usually did.

"I'll carry it," said Lucien, and he set off in the direction of the office.

"Hold on a minute," said Jacques, turning to Amélie. "Thanks, and I'll think about what you've said. I'll let Alain know, too."

Amélie smiled as she took her younger daughter's hand and guided her toward the car.

marseille, friday, june 7th, 17.05

Didier waited for the tram to take him down La Canebière to the old port, where he had a hired boat waiting for him. He could have walked from the car hire place to the port, but the four-hour drive had been tiring enough, and he just wanted to get to his temporary accommodation for the weekend as quickly as possible. He was looking forward to getting showered and changed and relaxing after travelling.

The whirr of the electric motor came closer as the tram approached. Didier jumped on and remained standing by the door. It was only four stops, and he wanted to feel the fresh air around him as the tram doors opened at each halt along the way. At the bottom of La Canebière he got off and strode across the wide busy street and on to Quai du Port. The *capitainerie* was right at the bottom, about half a kilometre away.

Registered for the weekend, and with the keys to his hired boat and the details of exactly where the vessel was moored, he retraced his steps to the last pontoon. The floating walkway stretched out at ninety degrees to the straight wall of the *quai* and towards the central sound of the harbour. It was perfectly positioned for the work he was required to do. As he drew towards his hired accommodation, Didier could see Sforza's yacht. It was berthed parallel to the mooring platform on the opposite side of the harbour, Rive Neuve, bow pointing towards the street along the harbour wall.

"Perfect," said Didier. "I've got a clear line of sight to the deck at the stern." He grinned. Turning to look at his own boat, he checked the lines at both the bow and the stern. Happy that everything was secure, he went aboard his comfortable but small floating home for the weekend.

mende, friday, june 7th, 17.15

"Where's Monsieur Didier?" Lucien asked as he dumped his backpack on the floor and started to pull out the contents and drop them anywhere.

"He's gone to Marseille for the weekend," said Jacques, eyeing the gradually-increasing mess.

"But I've drawn him a picture, *Papa*." Lucien produced a highly colourful rendering of a boat at sea with Didier at the helm.

Jacques grinned. "That's very good," he said, trying hard not to make mental comparisons with some of the artwork he'd been looking at over the past week. "Why don't you go through and say hello to Maxim and ask him nicely to help you stick it on Monsieur Didier's desk, so that he will see it when he comes in Monday?"

Lucien ran to the door.

"And come back straight away. I want to talk to you about something very important."

"OK, *Papa*." In a second, he was gone.

Jacques started to pack his bag ready to leave for the day. He picked up the open volume of the Vallade landscapes and snapped it shut. In a moment, it was in his bag and out of Lucien's sight, along with the three other books. Moving around the desk, he sat down and checked his emails one last time.

"All of that can wait, but I do need to download the will." He clicked on the document and saved it. Lucien raced back into the room as he was packing his laptop in his bag.

"I'm back," he announced as he plopped down on the sofa. Jacques went across and sat next to his son.

"Not everything stays the same, Lucien. You do understand that don't you?"

"Ah-ha."

"So, if I told you that next year, after school you may have to go somewhere else to wait for me to finish work, would you mind that?"

"Will Jeannette and Isabella be there as well?"

"They might be. I don't know yet."

"But Madame Amélie will be there, won't she? I like her games, *Papa*."

Jacques smiled. "No, I don't think so. Would it really matter to you if she wasn't there?"

Lucien frowned. "We sometimes play her games by ourselves, so I suppose we could do that." He looked to his left, towards his special corner of office space. "Can I still have my office?"

"Of course. That will be there for as long as you want it."

"OK," he said with a shrug. "Are we going home now?"

"Yes," said Jacques. As he got up to collect his bag and jacket, his phone rang. Pressing his finger to his lips to silence Lucien, he picked up the call.

"*Allo*, Jacques Foret…" He listened carefully. "OK, Madame Fribourg, I'll be there in ten minutes or so." Replacing his phone in his jacket pocket, Jacques hefted his bag onto his shoulder. The four art books weighed heavier than he thought they would.

"Get your bag, Lucien. We're leaving now."

Jacques went into the main office. "Maxim, I've had a call from Madame Fribourg. She thinks she's found something that might help us."

"OK. Do you need me to watch Lucien for you until you come back?"

Jacques hesitated. "No, it's OK, but thanks for the offer."

"What about these?" Maxim put his hand on a roll of papers. "The plans. The building owner dropped them off whilst you were at the school."

"I'll take them with me." Jacques collected the roll of blueprints and tucked them under his arm. "Have a good weekend."

"*Au revoir.*" Lucien waved as he followed his father out of the room.

Ten minutes later, Jacques was sitting in the small office at the back of the shop and gallery on rue du Soubeyran. Lucien was being given a guided tour of the three floors of paintings by Madame Fribourg's assistant.

The forged version of Vallade's painting was out of its frame and stood on the easel, the frame leaning against the wall.

"This is my drawing of the mark that I've found, Monsieur Forêt," she said, handing him a sheet of paper.

Jacques looked at it, nonplussed. He turned the paper to see if it made better sense upside down or sideways. It was still just as mystifying.

"So we have three points drawn as a complete line and then a single horizontal straight line through the centre, extending slightly on each side. Is it meant to mean something?"

"I don't know. But it was hidden on the back of the stretcher in the upper right corner." Madame Fribourg got up. She carefully lifted the painting off the easel and turned it around. "Right here," she said.

Jacques scrutinised the spot. The mark was barely visible to the naked eye. Jacques got out his phone. Once he had enlarged the mark on the screen, he clicked and got the shot.

Madame Fribourg replaced the painting on the easel. "And here's my photograph of the same spot on my original." She turned her laptop around so that Jacques could see the image.

"And this set of photographs was taken when?"

"Just three years ago."

Jacques looked at the photo he had just taken. "I can pass this on to an ex-colleague of mine who knows art and the fraud connected with it. He will—"

"No, Monsieur. I said no police. I want no taint of fraud or forgery connected with my picture or this gallery. I just want my property back."

"I understand that, Madame. But he may have come across this mark before, on other copies of works by other artists. He may already know of the forger, and I know he can be trusted. Please, just let me do my job."

Madame Fribourg picked up the frame and placed it on the table. "Alright," she said. Her reluctance was clearly visible on her face.

"I'll collect my son, and I hope you can enjoy your weekend, Madame."

Jacques left the stuffy little office and bounded up the stairs to the first floor. Lucien sat cross-legged on the floor, copying one of the sketches of the local cattle.

"He's a terrific little artist, isn't he?" The shop assistant held up a pencil drawing that Lucien had already completed.

"Yes, he is. Perhaps he will be famous one day. Thank you for looking after him, Madame. Lucien, come along."

"Just a minute, *Papa*. I want to finish the sky." His hand swiftly moved across the background with a pencil streaking the paper with broad stripes of pale blue.

"Would you like to be an artist when you grow up?"

"No. I want to be a vet like Monsieur Fabien," said Lucien putting his pencils in their case and then in his rucksack. "That one's for you, *Papa*."

"Thank you. I'll put it on the wall in my office."

Lucien scrambled to his feet and shouldered his rucksack. The assistant smiled and ushered them both out onto the street.

"Alright," said Jacques as he glanced at his watch. "I think it's time we went home."

mazargues, friday, may 10th, 19.26

At the small station of the *police municipale,* Madame Roşu and her daughter Elena waited in a cramped interview room. Sorina wasn't quite sure exactly who or what they were waiting for. Elena had done all the talking in her very rapid French, every so often turning to reassure her mother that everything was going to be sorted out, mostly whenever the officer had stepped out of the room for a moment or two. The more Madame Roşu thought about her situation, the more convinced she became that something had happened to her employer, Madame Apollinaire.

The police officer returned and ushered into the room a woman dressed in a similar style to Madame Roşu. He explained in French to Elena that the woman was an interpreter and that he would ask his questions, and the woman would translate. Madame Roşu could answer in her own tongue, and the answers would be relayed to the officer in French, who would write everything down.

Elena turned to her mother. "They are going to take your statement, *Mama,*" she said. "This lady will translate for you. It's standard procedure. Don't worry."

Sorina nodded and squeezed her daughter's hand.

The constant switching from one language to another made progress slow. But about an hour and a half later, the *gendarme* put his pen down.

"I'm happy with everything we have here," he said to Elena. "I just need your mother to sign this for me." He turned the papers round and indicated the points where a signature should go.

Madame Roşu took the offered pen from the *gendarme* and began the last piece of official business.

"Madame Apollinaire good lady. Kind lady," she said in her limited French as she scribbled her name. "Always pay. Wednesday and Friday. Always." With that, she stabbed at the statement with the point of the pen. She gave the *gendarme* a hard stare and a nod of her head just to let him know that the matter was of the utmost importance to her, and that despite the language barrier she was not to be messed with.

The policeman turned his attention to Elena. "I'm very sorry," he said. "But other than one individual breaking a private agreement with another..." He shrugged. "There is very little I can do. There is no formal contract of employment between Madame Apollinaire and your mother —"

"A verbal agreement to pay for work done, as is the situation here, can be argued to be a form of contract." Elena glared at the man across the table.

"In a court of law, perhaps. That is not here and not today. All I can see is an informal agreement between two parties that has failed. No laws have been broken."

"And the fact that Madame Apollinaire has disappeared?" Elena asked. "Is that of no interest to you at all?"

"From what you've told me, there is nothing here to indicate that Madame Apollinaire is anything other than away from home. She is free to go wherever she pleases. However," he gave a deep sigh. "I will check with missing persons to see if a close relative has reported her missing. That is all I can do."

The policeman collected his papers together and stood. "There really is nothing more I can do. So I suggest you take your mother home. If, when she goes back next week for her regular shift at the house or the studio and there is still no sign of Madame Apollinaire, come back to me. But I am sure everything will resolve itself." With that, he tucked his papers under his arm and opened the interview room door with a smile.

marseille, friday, june 7th, 20.02

The camera to secretly record the comings and goings on Sforza's yacht was in place. Didier had positioned it so that the deck on the vessel was in the centre of the picture, and had camouflaged it with the curtains of his cabin window. As the bow of the hired boat was facing east-south-east, he was confident that the tiny lens would not pick up and reflect any dwindling sunlight.

As he strolled down quai de Rive Neuve, he stopped to take a couple of photos just like any other tourist. And there were plenty around. The city was beginning to come alive again, as people came out to eat and meet friends or take advantage of the fresher air breezing in from the sea.

He wandered on towards the entrance to the port and took a few more shots. Turning to retrace his steps, he caught a glimpse of a colourful beanie hat as its owner made her way through the crowds.

"It can't be." He quickened his pace as he dodged around people, families, and groups of young people out for the night. He thought about shouting out, but there was too much noise. As he navigated his way through, he saw the small woman take a left into a backstreet. He followed. *It's her*.

"It's definitely her. I'd recognise those walking boots, those fatigues, that backpack and those dreadlocks anywhere." He strode out and managed to close the gap between them a little. At a bar in one of the streets that ran parallel to the harbour *quai*, she stopped at a table. Didier halted and watched. He grinned as both the young men gave her their change.

"Up to your old tricks again, Gaye." When she moved away, he followed. She turned into another narrow street a little further ahead. Didier continued behind her. When she mounted the steps to ascend to the road above, Didier sprinted up after her.

"*Bonsoir*, Gaye," he said as he drew level with her on the last-but-one step.

She looked up. In the half-light, she squinted. "It's *Duclos des flics*." A wide grin spread across her face. "This is a surprise. And what are you doing here?"

"I'm here for the weekend," he said. "A beer and a catch-up?"

A sly grin that Didier knew so well slid across her face. "Can I risk my reputation by having a drink with a married man?"

"Yes, you can," he said simply. "Annette died ten years ago. Cancer." He looked away.

"Oh, Didier," she said, a look of horror on her face. "I'm so sorry," she said, gently placing her hand on his arm. "I had no idea."

He shook his head. "It's OK," he said. "Everyone says that the pain gets easier. It doesn't, but I've noticed that you get better at covering it up as time moves on." He forced a smile.

Gaye grinned. "And yes, to the beer, the catch-up and something to eat. On you, of course."

"My pleasure," said Didier.

Gaye turned and set off to her left. "This way."

Didier matched his pace to hers as she led him through a maze of narrow streets to a small restaurant that served Turkish food.

"They know me here, and they're always good to me." She marched in and sat at a small table right at the back. Didier followed. "Are you still with *les flics*?"

"Not formally, no. I work for a private investigation firm now."

Gaye chuckled. "Still a copper then, but without the badge and the authority."

Didier smiled. "Something like that. What about you?"

Before she could answer, the waiter came to the table.

"Meze for four people, please."

"You've not changed!"

"I don't always know where my next meal is coming from, Didier."

"Are you living here now?"

"In the winter mostly, but I still move around a lot. Will be picking grapes in Hérault in September, and then I'll come back here. But I'm here this weekend because of the protest?"

"What protest?"

"The *Gilets Jaunes*. There's to be a big march right through the city tomorrow. Loads of cops drafted in, and whilst the cats are busy with crowd control, me and my friends will be out picketing the *Garde Forestier* and leafleting."

"Any particular reason?"

Gaye opened her backpack and pulled out a wodge of leaflets. "This," she said.

Didier picked up the top piece of paper. The photograph in the centre of the sheet was a tree that had been cut into, in exactly the same way as those on *Fermier* Sallan's property.

"We want the *Garde* and the rural *gendarmerie* to stop this happening. This is wanton destruction of perfectly healthy trees, and it's all for profit. And the *Garde* are doing nothing about it. They just accept that it is happening, and fell the damaged trees in place of others that they would have been cutting down anyway. They don't seem to understand that such a policy of tolerance is leading to more and more forested areas across the whole country being decimated like this."

"It's good to see you haven't lost any of your passion for a cause."

The waiter returned with two large trays of small dishes full of various bites to eat. The resulting aroma was both salty and sweet, spicy and aromatic all at once. Didier breathed it in.

"This looks good," he said.

"It is." Gaye immediately began filling her small plate

with tasty morsels from a range of dishes. "These are really delicious," she said, helping herself to what looked like some sort of cocktail sausages. "Come on, Didier, get stuck in."

He began to help himself to various pieces of food, just one of each, until he came to the dish that Gaye had pointed out. He took two of the sausages and tried one of them first.

"No!" But it was too late. Didier's face showed that the hot spice was a bit too much. "You're supposed to gradually work up to the hottest dishes," she said.

Didier gulped down some of his beer. "I've never eaten Turkish food before," he said, as if that excused every other mistake he would make during the rest of their shared banquet.

"You know, Gaye, you might be able to help me out with something," he said as he paused for a moment before attempting one of the other dishes.

"Will it pay?"

Didier grinned. "It can do, if your terms are still your usual ones."

"They never change, Didier. Never will."

"I was called out to a farm a few kilometres south of Mende yesterday. In a small copse, five trees had been damaged exactly as shown on your leaflet. A couple of them were hundreds of years old."

Gaye stilled, a morsel of food halfway to her open mouth. "That's sacrilege," she said.

"I know. I was stunned when I saw the damage." He pulled out his phone and scrolled through his gallery for the sequence of shots of the ancient chestnut.

When she looked up, there were tears in her eyes. "How can anyone do that?"

You still feel everything so deeply. "Some insight into where the wood is going or where it's being sold would be helpful."

"North Africa," she said without hesitation. "It's cut into easily-handleable chunks and smuggled to North Africa, where it's carved into trinkets, book-ends, coasters, jewellery and that sort of stuff. All for the tourist trade where the items are sold at ridiculous prices to selfish people who don't give a shit about the ecological murder they are helping to fund."

Didier frowned. "I shouldn't ask this, but you and your tree-hugging friends, might you be passing through Mende in the next week or so?"

Gaye grinned. "I think that can be arranged. What sort of protest did you have in mind?"

"I don't have anything in mind, Gaye and I can't really be seen to be involved in any way. But I'm sure you can come up with something suitable."

"Leave it to me, Didier." She raised her hand to attract the waiter's attention.

As two more beers arrived, Didier drained the last of his and handed over his empty glass.

"You said you were here for the weekend," Gaye prompted as she started to add more food to her plate. "But you didn't say why."

Didier shrugged. "It's for work. I can't talk about it."

"But you're going back when?"

"Early Monday morning. And yes, you can count on me to foot the bill for dinner tomorrow and Sunday."

"Great, thanks, Didier."

"However, tomorrow we will have aperitifs on the boat I've hired, and it would look much better if you scrubbed up a bit and wore a dress. I suppose you have still got one, haven't you?"

Gaye had a wide grin on her face. "This sounds intriguing. I haven't been a decoy for you for years!"

"The rules haven't changed, Gaye, and it will be the same scenario. Errant daughter visiting her dad. Got it?"

"Got it." She tucked into some mixed red cabbage and carrot dressed in mayonnaise that reminded Didier of slaw. He decided it wasn't for him. "What time, and where?"

Didier pulled out his notebook, scribbled down the details, ripped out the page, and handed it to her. He drained the last of his beer and called the waiter over.

"The bill, please."

"Am I allowed to ask who we'll be watching... whilst not watching, of course," she added after a beat.

"No. As I said, all the usual rules still apply."

"You're just no fun, Didier."

The waiter returned. Didier glanced at the number at the bottom, took out his wallet and placed two twenty-euro notes on the dish, which the waiter whisked away.

"*À demain*," he said as he rose from his chair. "And don't be late."

Gaye nodded.

In the next minute, Didier was outside on the street, wondering how he would find his way back to the port. On a whim, he headed left. It was a beautiful evening, the sun hadn't quite set, and the intensity of the day's heat had been eroded by the slightly cooler breeze from the sea.

mende, friday, june 7th, 21.48

Jacques had the plans for the gallery laid out on the table in the dining area. He'd examined each and every floor. The fire escape was at the back of the building, and there was one point of access on all four floors. The plan for the third floor showed that there was access to the roof area by means of some stairs, but as Jacques mentally walked through his memory of the space, he was at a loss to pinpoint where that extra staircase might be. Other than the windows and the staircase down to the other floors, there seemed to be no other way out from the Vallade display room. When he closed his eyes and pictured the room, he could only see pictures on the walls between the windows. He would need to go back and look at the building with the plans as a direct comparison.

"And I think I'll take Didier with me," he decided as he put the plans on top of one another, with the third-floor blueprint uppermost.

Moving out on to the balcony with a glass of beer he slumped down on the lounger. What was wrong with Lucien, he wondered. Reading the bedtime story was something that Jacques had always enjoyed. But tonight, that simple pleasure had been denied him when Lucien suddenly announced that he would read his story himself. *Is parenting always this confusing?* He shook the thought away, deciding he would mention it to his sister the next time he called her.

He resumed his reading about Charles-Marcel Vallade. Chapter Seven explored the artist's time in America and the new influences on his work. It was clear that Vallade had been experimenting with colour and medium. During this period, some of his work became controversial as it was interpreted as adverse comment on commercialism and the great American dream. Jacques noted that the quote at the head of the chapter was dated 1957. *That has to be from one of Professor Simmonet's letters.*

THE AMERICAN YEARS: 1938-1946

I went into the marriage with nothing but my raw talent. I expected little from it, and I certainly had no desire for children. Nevertheless, when my son was born I could do nothing other than love him... His death was a terrible blow. It set a cloud on the marriage from which neither of us recovered. I left with nothing but my talent...

—Charles-Marcel Vallade, 1957

The years in America were a significant turning point for Vallade. He was barely known over there, and those that did recognise his work did so through his portraiture. He found he spent more time in drawing rooms and at society events than before his canvasses. His output slowed, and was mostly confined to portraits.

His opportunities to take time out to paint landscapes became rarer, and he came to dislike living in the city of New York. His one exhibition in Manhattan during this period closed early, because the critics saw a European commenting on American ideals. Shortly afterwards, his only son drove his motorbike off a cliff just days before his eighteenth birthday.

The mood and colour palette of Vallade's work following his son's death assumed a darker and sombre tone. The subject-matter became more harrowing. Eventually he stopped painting. The final breakdown of his crumbling marriage came in 1944, the legal disentanglement taking a further year and a half to be settled.

There were few new landscapes during this period, but the panels and oils discussed here clearly chart Vallade's descent into emotional turmoil. A direct comparison between **L208** *City Skyline* (completed in 1945) and **L183** *Central Park* (completed in 1938) show a marked shift in colour, tone and brushwork, with his works in between becoming more critical of American life through the subjects featured. **L197** *Central Park at Dusk* (completed in 1944) shows a group of three homeless men juxtaposed with the wealthy. His portraiture in Volume Two, however, shows a much starker and deeper descent, and this is discussed in much more detail there.

mende, saturday, june 8th, 10.12

Jacques strolled into place Urbain V. The market was already full of people. The hustle and bustle of the crowds and the noise of the traders as they made offers to passing customers would have been enough to drown out the basilica's bells had they still been able to sound.

Sauntering left and right, Jacques kept alert, looking for the man with the toy dogs. He was also looking for any rogue traders that might be selling timber. Having reasoned that it would be a long shot that whoever stole the wood from *Fermier* Sallan would sell it locally, still, he couldn't stop himself. There seemed to be nothing else he and Didier could do to help identify the perpetrators. A conviction wouldn't save the farmer's trees or recover the loss of income if he'd sold his wood, but it would bring the satisfaction of justice.

Further into the market, Jacques saw a small table with a cloth that looked like the one he'd seen at the *kermesse*. He strolled over. The man behind the table was the vendor he'd seen before. As Jacques approached, something familiar caught his eye. When he looked to his right, all he could see were shoppers. He felt sure he'd caught a brief glimpse of sunlight in a lens. He dismissed it. *It could have been a reflection in the plate glass of a window.*

Jacques approached the man and looked at the table, which had nothing but a few dog leads, some dog blankets, and other bits and pieces for the family pet.

"Monsieur, you had some of the toy dogs before."

"They're out of stock," the vendor said.

"Will you be getting any more?"

The man shrugged. "It's possible," he said.

"In the next week or month?"

"It's possible," repeated the man. Jacques frowned. The lack of information was troubling.

"And how much are they?"

"Thirty or forty euros," he said. "It depends how big they are."

"A couple of weeks ago, I saw you had a white dog with tan-coloured ears. Might you be able to get one like that?"

"Yes, that one was a terrier," he said. "I can try and get you one if you want. But it will take about a week."

"OK, said Jacques. Do I pay you now?"

The man shook his head. "I may not be able to get one. Write your number down," he said, offering Jacques a scrap of paper and a pen. "I will contact you when I've got one."

"OK, thanks. I hope to hear from you soon." Jacques moved away, and again he felt the sensation of being watched. He looked around, but there were still only other shoppers to be seen.

He strolled through the market and eventually returned to his office, where he had left the car. As he stepped along the side of the building to make his way into the underground car park, he saw *Gendarme* Lefèvre walking towards him.

"*Bonjour*, Lefèvre. Plain clothes? Or not on duty today?"

"Jacques. *Ça va*. I'm on duty, and I need to talk to you. Can we use your office?"

"The car's nearer. It's just in here." Jacques pointed to the meshed roller door across the entrance. He keyed in the code, and the door began to rise.

"What's this about?" Jacques ducked under the receding roll of metal.

"The man you were talking to at the market. We're watching him."

"So I didn't imagine it. I had a feeling something was going on."

"We've been looking for him for a while, but he keeps going to ground. Can I ask what you were talking about?"

As Jacques reached his car, he clicked the fob for the central locking and got in behind the wheel. Lefèvre got in the passenger side.

"That vendor was at the *kermesse* in Messandrierre over the holiday weekend, and he had some toy dogs in little baskets. I wanted to know if he would be getting any more. But if you're watching him, then he must be involved in something illegal."

"He is," said Lefèvre. "Illegal trade in animals. Specifically dogs. Puppies are being brought in from eastern Europe. Mostly from breeders who are not appropriately licensed in their own countries."

Jacques ran his hands through his hair. "I think you'd better tell me the worst."

"It's not good, Jacques. Those 'toys' are the skins of real puppies that died in transit, and once they're stuffed and stitched into a cheap dog-basket, they can fetch anything from thirty to sixty euros. It's not as much as the traders would get for a live puppy in Paris, but it's something, and as far as they're concerned, something is better than nothing."

Jacques suddenly felt physically sick. "I just need a minute," he said as he got out of the car and took a lung full of air.

Lefèvre got out too. "OK?"

Jacques nodded.

"Have you made some sort of agreement with the trader?"

Jacques nodded. "He's going to contact me when he's got a terrier, and—" He couldn't finish his sentence. The contents of his stomach were suddenly and violently spread on the concrete of the car park floor. He reached into the door's pocket and took out a small bottle. "Excuse me," he said to Lefèvre, and gulped back half the water. "You're going to want me to go through with this, aren't you?"

"Only if you want to, Jacques. Otherwise, you can come into the station and make a statement, and we can leave it at that. It'll be valuable evidence from a reputable source, and will help us build our case."

Jacques leaned on the roof of the car. "He's going to ring me. I'll let you know as soon as he does, and then you can pick him up, along with the further evidence, at the same time."

"Thanks, Jacques." Lefèvre turned to leave. "If you've got time today to make that statement, it would help."

Jacques checked his watch. "I can't really. I've got to get to the swimming baths to pick up Lucien. I'll come in on Monday."

Lefèvre nodded and strode out of the car park.

Jacques got back in the car and started the engine. "I knew there was something suspect about that man," he said as he reversed out of his parking spot.

marseille, saturday, june 8th, 11.38

Didier had spent almost two hours traipsing around the city's northern quarter, and was now heading to the last address on his list. So far, his hunch had been wrong. At face value, all the other establishments in Sfoza's portfolio were legitimate businesses. As he'd visited each one, he recognised that they could be acting as cover for other things, but it seemed unlikely. The women's hairdressers, the nail bar, and the café all seemed to be doing well and were packed with what looked like genuine customers.

"So what is Sforza's angle?" The question had been going through his head all morning, and asking it out loud had not provided any answers. *Unless it's money-laundering.* He kept coming back to that unsatisfactory conclusion.

The final property was on a street corner, all shuttered, the grey steel liberally covered with graffiti. Didier looked up to the second and third storeys. All the windows were as shuttered, grey and graffitied as those on the ground floor. He banged on the shutter for the only door. There was no response. Walking further down the street, he saw an alleyway that went behind the building. He checked it out. A small yard sat at the back of the property. The only door at this side was shuttered, as were the windows, apart from a tiny window on the top floor that contained a pane of dirty frosted glass. From that, there came a very faint light. As Didier was about to turn and leave, one of the large fans on the exterior of the building began to spin.

Didier quickly left the yard and moved across the road, took some photos of the location and disappeared along the street. Walking briskly, he made his way back to the nearest bus stop and took the first vehicle towards the city centre.

The bus dropped him at the railway station. It was a short walk across the city to Canebière, and from there a ten-minute brisk walk to the port. He'd decided that lunch would be light today and eaten alone on the boat.

Once aboard, Didier was anxious to see the video recordings of Sforza's yacht. He retrieved his laptop, logged in and started scanning the recording. There had been quite a bit of movement on and off the boat, but no indication that Sforza was there. The chef and a couple of other people had arrived whilst Didier was in the northern quarter. The video showed a suited man arriving and taking up a position on the rear deck just before he returned.

Didier zoomed in on his face. "You'll be Sforza's heavy man, I expect." *And if all your businesses are legit, Monsieur Sforza, why do you need a heavy man?* Didier stared at the face. It was hard, and he recognised there would be no compromising with that man. He clicked through to the look-up application and pasted in the face. He left the application running whilst he prepared and ate his lunch.

At just after two, Sforza arrived at the yacht: a tall man in a sharp suit, open-neck shirt and carrying a briefcase. Didier watched from his deck as Sforza removed his jacket and talked to the first man who had arrived. Didier went below and checked that the camera was still running.

Back on deck, he waited until he was sure Sforza would be remaining aboard. Confident that his target was settled for the afternoon, Didier locked up his boat and left. He picked up a taxi and instructed the driver to follow the coast road south out of the city and along the promontory towards Cap Croisette. The driver did not need to know that Didier's destination was Sforza's villa on the city's outskirts.

At the last hamlet on the shoreline, Didier asked the driver to stop. He paid him and then started out on foot. According to his map, boulevard Mont-Rose was about four hundred metres ahead. Didier kept walking until he came to the very last property. A large white-painted house surrounded by white-painted walls. The entrance was a full-height metal gate with an intercom. Didier slowed his pace as he passed.

"Tight security. CCTV and cameras on the house too." The first floor had floor-to-ceiling windows overlooking the sea. Didier turned and scanned the view. "No need to guess why this is here," he said as his gaze took in the islands where the Château d'If was located, and in the distance the coastline to the west of the city.

The road before him began to rise, and Didier kept walking. He hoped he might be able to get enough height to see over the walls of the villa. Another five hundred metres further on, and his view of the house was little improved. He took a few shots and then headed back to the village's centre. Hopefully, he could find a taxi somewhere.

messandrierre, saturday, june 8th, 14.09

"I can see a ship," shouted Lucien as he pointed to a cloud over the trees on his right.

"I can see a witch," replied Jacques pointing in the opposite direction. "Your turn." The grass of the small patch of lawn, having been in the lee of the chalet, was cool on his back as he watched the clouds shifting in shape and shade.

"I can see... a bug!"

"No, that's not specific enough. What sort of bug?"

"The head of a mantis."

Jacques scanned the sky but couldn't see anything even faintly resembling the particular shape of the head of a praying mantis.

"I think you're cheating," he said, rolling over and tickling his son's tummy. Lucien squealed with delight and fell into a fit of giggles.

Jacques glanced at his watch and sat upright. "That's enough for today. Come on. We need to get cleaned up, and then I'll walk with you over to Danielle's house."

Lucien scrambled to his feet and started running to the door. "Last one there's a mouse."

Jacques shook his head and just quickened his pace. "I would have thought you'd have grown out of that by now," he muttered. "Get washed and don't forget to do your teeth. And I've put your pale brown trousers and your checked shirt on the bed for you. OK?" Jacques shouted to Lucien as he ran up the spiral staircase to his room.

Twenty minutes later, Jacques bounded up the stairs. "Lucien, we're going to be late if you don't hurry up."

Lucien was sitting on the bed staring at his brown lace-up shoes in his room. He padded out onto the sitting area of the loft and pulled a face.

"What's the matter?"

"I want to wear my new trainers," he whined.

"You're going to a birthday party, Lucien. That means you have to make a special effort. Now, put your smart brown shoes on, please."

"Are you wearing your proper shoes too?"

Jacques glanced at his loafers. "Yes," he lied. "Shoes on, and come down as soon as you can."

Downstairs, Jacques went straight to the boot room and changed into his lace-ups. As he came back into the main living space, Lucien jumped from the third step onto the floor and landed with a solid thud.

"Alright," said Jacques. "Birthday present?"

Lucien dithered, shot through to the dining area, and pulled a neatly-wrapped square box from the top of the table.

"Let's go." Pulling the front door closed, Jacques locked it, and they both marched down the path and into the village.

saturday, june 8th, 15.02

Audrey Taillard the *avocat* looked far more formidable on camera than in the black and white photograph on her business page. As soon she was connected into the video call, Madame Taillard immediately took control of the conversation.

"Monsieur Forêt, hello. May I call you Jacques?"

"Of course."

"Thank you. I've been reviewing the evidence and all the arguments presented by your mother-in-law's solicitor. I'm sorry, but there's no nice way to say this. The core of their case is that you are not fit to remain as the sole parent for Lucien."

"No! No, I'm not accepting that," shouted Jacques. "I've cared for my son since he was a few months old. My wife had a serious car accident which left her in a persistent vegetative state. She... erm she, she died last year." He cleared his throat.

"I'm sorry to hear that, but it does raise a question. Why has Madame Williams decided to take this action now?"

"I think it is what she has always wanted. But for as long as Beth was still alive with the hope of recovery, no matter how remote, Madame Williams just waited. When I informed her of the accident, she announced then that she would seek custody of Lucien. But of course, at that point, none of us knew whether Beth would make it through the hours immediately following the crash. I refused to accept that custody belonged to Beth's mother. As difficult as I knew it would be, I still refused. I also wanted to protect Beth. She would never have forgiven me if she had recovered fully and found Lucien gone."

"You said difficult. How difficult has it been thus far?"

"I was talking about practicalities, not about Lucien himself. He's an easy child in comparison with some of the stories I hear from the other parents at the school gates. But the greatest difficulty has been the practicalities of having a baby to look after and a business that doesn't really run on regular hours. When Lucien was born, I took a whole month off from the job and left my colleague, Didier Duclos, to handle all aspects of the business."

"There must be a great level of trust between you."

"There is. There always has been. We don't agree on everything, of course, but we're personal friends and now business partners. We know we can trust each other with our lives in a tight situation."

"How did you overcome the day-to-day practical difficulties?"

"We created a *crêche* at the office, and Amélie, the wife of one of my team members who also have children, ran the *crêche* just for Lucien and their two girls. After the accident, I took another three months off work to look after Lucien, ensure Beth was properly cared for and to put everything necessary in place for the childcare facility at the office. Once Lucien started school, things became a little easier, but we still have the *crêche*, which has become the after-school club, and occasionally Amélie will bring other children to the club, for which their parents pay an hourly fee. Lucien and I do everything together. I've built my working and personal lives around my son and what's best for him. But he has his little friends at school that he spends time with. He's at a birthday party this afternoon, which is why I'm free to talk to you."

"Does that mean Lucien knows nothing of the residency order?"

"Yes. I don't want him unsettled by this, and I've decided only to explain what is happening if and when it becomes necessary. I'm hoping that we will never reach that point."

"I see." Madame Taillard made a note. When she looked up at the screen again, a deep frown was on her forehead. "I can work with that, Jacques, but if it becomes necessary for me to talk to Lucien, how will you explain who I am and why I need to talk to him?"

"Why would you need to speak to my son?"

"To get his point of view on living with his dad."

"So, perhaps, I could introduce you as an old friend."

"Yes, that would work to start with, but you need to prepare for the fact that Lucien may have to be present at any possible hearings."

Jacques grimaced and pulled his thumb and forefinger across his eyes. "I'll deal with that if and when I have to," he said.

"OK. So to the evidence and arguments. The central argument surrounds your business. You're a private investigator. The hours, by your own admission, are not regular, so how do you balance work and the life of a small child?"

"We have the after-school club, which Lucien enjoys. He also has a small space of his own in my office. He attends various activities after school. He goes swimming one day a week, on Tuesdays, and is a member of the children's swimming club that meets once a month on a Saturday. He also attends a creative arts club once a week on Wednesdays. He used to attend a cycling club on a Saturday, but he's passed all the tests now. I drop him off at school on Mondays and Fridays and collect him each evening. On the other days of the week, Amélie takes him to and picks him up from school or his after-school activity."

"And if you need to work late?"

"I don't. I take Lucien home, we eat, he plays or does any homework or prep for school, and then he goes to bed. Any work I need to complete gets done after he's asleep."

"I've checked your website, Jacques. You offer a range of services including house-sitting. How does that work with your responsibilities as a parent?"

"I always take the day shifts, with my colleagues handling the night and evening shifts. I have some casual staff that I can and do call on for those sorts of commissions. I always put Lucien first."

"Your work won't stop at weekends, will it? How do you manage that?"

"In exactly the same way. I put Lucien first. He has play dates with friends every so often, and when he does, I'm able to handle some work during his absence. Often it's research on the internet, occasionally an interview with someone connected with a case, but whatever the work, it's never done at Lucien's expense."

"Are you certain of that?"

"Yes. Why do you think this conversation had to be at this time today? And," he held up his mobile phone and placed it close to the camera. "Why do you think I have an alarm set on my phone that says *Pick up Lucien*? It's not because I cannot remember to pick up my son from wherever he is. It's because I want to make sure we reach the end of our conversation before I need to leave. It's vital that Lucien knows I will be waiting for him when the party finishes. And if our conversation is not complete, we will arrange another time and date. I will not ignore that alarm, Madame Taillard."

The *avocat* nodded. "OK," she said at last. "You're very organised, Monsieur. Time is pressing, so can I move on to some instances of Lucien's bad behaviour? Mrs Williams has cited—"

"Bad behaviour? What bad behaviour?"

The *avocat* sifted through some pages. "Christmas last year, Monsieur. According to Madame Williams, Lucien wouldn't eat his food. He sulked and threw a tantrum when he realised that he had to wait until Christmas Day to open his presents."

"No," said Jacques, his tone hard and forceful. "That is a complete misrepresentation of what happened. Madame Williams has misremembered the whole thing. It was her other grandchild who misbehaved. Not Lucien. I was there. I saw and heard it all."

"Does Madame Williams often misremember things? I note from the information I have that she will be seventy-five in a couple of months or so."

Jacques thought for a moment. "Yes, that's right. But I don't think she misremembers things any more frequently than other people of her age. But she has a great capacity for re-inventing incidents to suit her purpose."

"Do you have an example of that?"

Jacques let out a gasp. "I can't think... No, I do have something. She told her son Matthew that I had withheld details of Beth's funeral to ensure that none of Beth's family could be there. That was not true. I didn't withhold anything. I deliberately asked if the funeral could be delayed to ensure that Beth's family could get there in time. As soon as I had a date and time I told Madame Williams."

"OK. Going back to Christmas. What does Lucien think about Christmas in England?"

"He's happy with it. Before he was born, when Beth was pregnant, we agreed that we would make sure that Lucien was taught both English and French customs. We agreed that we would ensure that he was bi-lingual. I have kept to the agreement even though Beth has not been here to help me..." Jacques cleared his throat and remained silent for a few moments. "Since we were together, Beth and I have always had a French Christmas one year and an English Christmas the following year. When Lucien came along, I just continued in the same way."

Madame Taillard smiled. "He's a fortunate little boy."

"Thank you." Conscious of time, Jacques glanced at his watch.

"I want to move onto something else that Madame Williams has cited. She states that she believes your working environment is not healthy for a small boy. She states that you associate with known criminals and that you have been shot twice."

Jacques shook his head. "I can't believe she is dragging up such old information. I was in the police force in Paris, Madame. I was a detective. In 2007, before I even knew Beth existed, I was working undercover on a case, and I was injured whilst on duty. It was a gunshot wound to my left shoulder. Whilst I was convalescing, I re-evaluated my life and my work. I decided to get out of the city and join the rural *gendarmerie* here. In 2011, whilst following through on a private investigation, I received a flesh wound in my arm. It was nothing. I do not associate with criminals, Madame. But as an ex-policeman, I have come across a few criminals because of my work. I don't see how I could have avoided that."

"Quite. What about long-term, Jacques? Is the business providing enough regular income for you to provide security for Lucien now and in the future?"

That's the one question I really don't want to answer. He wondered if he should lie or perhaps just gloss over the state of the business finances.

"Not at the moment, no," he said, finally deciding on being completely honest. "We have been just about breaking even for a while now. I've introduced efficiencies and added new services to our portfolio. We are beginning to see a slow uptake of new cases. So I'm hopeful for the future. But if I have to give up the investigation business, then I will do that. Lucien's welfare is my most important priority."

"OK, Jacques. I think I have enough for the moment, so I'll let you collect your son, and I'll be in touch in a few days when I've decided what our strategy should be."

"Thank you."

mazargues, saturday, may 11th, 18.19

The duty officer tossed the file of papers he'd spent most of the afternoon working on into a tray and sat back.

"Case closed," he said to his computer, the sound of relief in his voice noticeable only to himself. He moved through various screens adding information and clicking boxes until he was content he had covered everything. He pushed his chair away from the desk and stretched. It had been a long day. Removing his spectacles, he rubbed his knuckles into his closed but tired eyes. It was only as he looked up again that he saw the statement from the previous week: Madame Roşu's statement. He pulled it out of the tray, reread it, and still could not decide what to do with it.

"An employer who doesn't pay, well, that's a civil matter, isn't it?" He glanced down at the detail of the text. "No formal employment contract," he noted. He looked again at the address of the place of work. Boulevard des Anges. Something about that street name struck a chord in his memory. Quickly flicking back over the details recorded, he remembered his promise to check with missing persons.

"Did I make that call?" A frown crossed his forehead, and he pulled out his notebook and checked the last few pages. And there it was at the top of the second page. A cryptic note that his colleagues on missing persons had come up blank. Wondering if he should treat the report as that of a missing person rather than a missing wage packet, he reminded himself that he had very few details. Madame Roşu had not been able to tell him if the name Apollinaire was a family name, a given name or some form of a nickname. It was just an odd name. Eventually, he picked up the phone and called a colleague.

"Francis, it's Raoul... The unidentified dead female

you've got in the morgue… Yes, that's right, the one found at the end of boulevard des Anges. Any progress?"

No, came the response.

"And remind me, that street is here in the ninth, isn't it? What about house-to-house enquiries?"

He listened carefully and jotted down some notes. "And the pathologist's report?"

He continued to make notes as he listened. "Hang on, let me get that down," he said as he scribbled a note. "Time of death between 23.00 on May 1st and 01.00 on May 2nd," he repeated and paused in thought. "Just a minute…" Raoul quickly flicked through the statement again. "Ah, yes," he said. "Paid on the first but not on the eighth. That might fit, Francis. What about the cause of death?"

Raoul listened intently and scribbled yet more notes. "A sharp narrow blade pushed under the rib cage directly into the heart. That sounds like a contract killing to me." He paid close attention as his colleague went through all the salient points connected with the death. "Just let me get that down… She was found with no ID, no keys, no money, handbag, phone or jewellery and the… What?"

Raoul listened and let out a low whistle. "Fingertips dipped in acid? It's a long time since I've come across that one." He waited as his colleague talked at length, jotting down names and dates.

"Thanks, Francis. I'll look up those other cases. What I can't get my head around is that managing to strip a body of jewellery and all forms of ID takes time. And to be carrying around enough acid to burn off the fingerprints… That takes some doing, and if the street is where I think it is, that's a quiet residential area. There must have been at least two perpetrators to carry out the crime, and probably a third to keep watch. And they would be—"

Francis's interruption brought a deep frown to Raoul's face. "OK," he said. "Thanks, and if you can, let me have a copy of the pathologist's report and the tox screen information as well." Raoul made the odd note as his colleagued talked.

"Of the addresses where you're still waiting for people to get in touch, do any householders use the name Apollinaire?" Raoul listened.

"I don't know," said Raoul in response to his colleague's question. "It could be either a first or a family name or even a nickname, but it's the only name I've got." Raoul waited while his colleague on the other end of the line had a conversation with someone else before returning to the current call.

"So, the addresses on the street where you've had no response, can you let me have them?" Raoul grabbed a sheet of paper and a pen and quickly scribbled down four addresses as his colleague rattled them off.

"Yeah… Thanks, Francis."

Raoul placed his phone on his desk. "That's a contract killing," he said to himself. He picked up the statement from Madame Roşu and stared at it. "But why would an artist from Mazargues be the subject of a contract killing?" He slapped the papers back in his tray. "It doesn't make sense," he muttered as he picked up his phone and made a second call to his colleagues in Missing Persons.

"A possible missing person, adult, female, around thirty years of age, with either a first or family name of Apollinaire. You got anything that might fit?" Raoul drummed his fingers on the desk as he waited for a response.

"Yep. Definitely Apollinaire… Really? I can't say I've come across his work before… OK… What? No, I'm just covering all bases. I don't think I've got much here other than a private dispute over pay in a private employment situation… Yes, that's right, no formal work contract…" Raoul let out a bellow of a laugh. "I know. I did wonder if either or both parties were declaring the situation to the tax office. But that's a whole other minefield, and I don't want to go there, either figuratively or literally. But it's the leap that the witness has made from missing wages to missing person that keeps coming back to haunt me. It's a big jump, but this lady was so sure that something had happened to her Madame Apollinaire…"

After a few final pleasantries, Raoul ended the call and put the phone on the desk.

"Early-twentieth-century poet! Well, that's just what I need." He scooped up his remaining notes and papers and shoved them in his drawer. Putting his phone in his pocket and collecting his jacket and cap, he got up. It had been a long week, and a dead poet was just the final straw. Raoul left. His next shift wasn't until Tuesday, and he was going to make the most of his weekend.

Just as he got out onto the street, Raoul spun around. He should have asked for a photo of the victim from the morgue. He could show that to Madame Roşu, and if she recognised the body, his case was closed, and the detectives could handle it from there. There might even be a few beers in it for him, for providing them with a possible identification.

marseille, saturday, june 8th, 19.06

With the few nibbles he'd bought at a shop in one of the side streets, and a chilled bottle of rosé in the fridge in the tiny galley, Didier could be doing what every other boatman would be doing all along the pontoons in the port: enjoying the Friday evening sunshine with an *aperitif*. He checked his watch. *Gaye should be here very soon.* He went below deck to check the camera and to collect a couple of glasses.

As he came back up, he saw Gaye walking along the pontoon. He waved to her and stepped off the boat to greet her.

"This is very nice," she said, kissing him on both cheeks.

"And you've scrubbed up pretty well."

"Dress and sunhat borrowed, sandals five euros at a *vide-grenier*."

Didier grinned. "Let's have a drink. Is a rosé OK for you?"

Gaye nodded, stepped onto the boat and made herself comfortable. As Didier poured the wine, he saw Alain Vaux arrive with his wife and join their host on his boat. Sforza came out on deck to meet them. The two men shook hands. The amicability of the commonplace gesture was undermined by the mask of controlled emotion on the face of one and the narrowed-eyed distrust on the face of the other.

Didier offered a glass to Gaye and then sat opposite her. He didn't want Alain to see him.

"So, who are we watching?" Gaye glanced around at the numerous craft.

"Never you mind. Just behave as though you are enjoying catching up with your dad."

"That would be a first," she said. "I've always thought

that, if it were possible to choose your parents, I would have chosen you and Annette," she said. "You both looked after me far better than anyone else I've ever met."

Didier grinned. "Thanks. We just did what was right. I can see you still live rough, but you are still clean, aren't you?"

"Yes. Getting me through rehab, supporting me afterwards... Best thing you and Annette could have done for me. Best thing anyone's done. And I get proper rooms when I can, but my constant travelling doesn't always sit well with that."

On the pretence of getting up to get some more nibbles, Didier stood. As he ducked below deck, he looked across the sound to Sforza's yacht. Now there were six people on deck, with Sforza in the centre of the group, all chatting. Didier came back.

"We'll finish these," he said, nodding to their glasses. "And then we'll get something to eat. I'd like to visit a good seafood restaurant just along the *quai*."

"I'll eat anything," she said, clinking her glass with his.

Returning to his boat, Didier looked across the sound as he traversed the walkway. Only Sforza's bodyguard seemed to be on board.

"The party has moved elsewhere," he said as he unlocked the entrance to the cabin. Once aboard, he went straight to the camera. It was still running.

Logging onto his laptop, he started to work through the results of the look-up searches he'd set running the previous evening. The first few results revealed photos and attendant articles he'd already found. Searching a little further down the list, and specifically looking for information more than five years old, he found a couple of new items. He clicked on the first.

A newspaper article came on screen. The text was Cyrillic, and Didier couldn't read a word. But the photograph that went with it was easy enough to understand. There was a coffin surrounded by mourners, and one of those in attendance was a young Milo Sforza.

Didier stared at the screen. "I reckon you're about fourteen or fifteen years of age there." Beside him was a much older man. "Grandfather perhaps?"

He clicked on the *Translate* button in the top right-hand corner of the screen and started reading. After a few minutes, he saved the article to his hard drive.

Armed with a name for the young boy in the photograph, Didier did an internet-wide search. Numerous items came up, including an article about a conviction for money-laundering and details of a custodial sentence.

"So I was right all along," he told himself. "Always trust your gut."

Turning his attention to the video footage he'd collected, he returned to the start of the evening. Copying and pasting the faces of all those present into his look-up application, he set that running. In the meantime, he texted Jacques.

> Sforza not what he seems. Real name Mikhail Miloslavsky. Has conviction for money-laundering. Am running a look-up on the others at an event yesterday. Driving back tomorrow. Got news on trees.

messandrierre, saturday, june 8th, 22.18

Jacques pinched the bridge of his nose with his thumb and forefinger. His eyes were tired from reading all the detail of Vallade's will and the attendant papers relating to the Trust. Gleaning the crucial elements from the documents had been difficult. When his phone pinged with a message from Didier, he was glad of the distraction. He video-called his colleague.

"Didier, thanks for the update. Alain's suspicions were right, I think."

"Yes, Jacques," Didier said after taking a sip of rosé. "There's more. I checked out his business properties, and they all looked legitimate apart from one. He has a four-storey building, a corner plot that's completely shuttered up and looks as though it hasn't been used for years. But there was a faint light from a small window on the fourth floor, and a fan on the external back wall that was working."

Jacques grinned. "And why would an empty building need ventilation?"

"I still think it could be drugs," said Didier. "His property on the city's outskirts is substantial, with a panoramic view of the Med and top-notch security. That villa and the yacht shout money and plenty of it."

"Does Alain know yet?"

"I've held off contacting him until tomorrow as I'm not sure whether he is still with Sforza or not."

"OK. You said you'd got something on the tree investigation."

"Yes, I bumped into an old nark. She was here because of the protest in the city earlier today. According to her, the wood is used to craft items for the tourist industry and mostly ends up in North Africa."

"OK. When we're back in the office next week, I think we need to agitate the local police and the *Garde*. And can you make sure *Fermier* Sallan makes a statement, please?"

"I was planning on calling out to see him anyway, Jacques. I believe he deserves to know what has happened to his wood. I think that if he understands the level of destruction he's seen is to fund trinkets, he will insist that the police investigate fully."

"And this old informant of yours. Can her information be trusted?"

Didier nodded. "It can, Jacques. I first came across her when I was investigating a case in St Étienne. Gaye was fifteen years old and half-dead from a cache of bad pills that were on the street. I got her into rehab, and Annette supported her afterwards. Then she just gradually disappeared from our lives, until about five or six years later. Gaye tracked me down to the station in Mende because she had some important information. It led us to the evidence and the conviction we were looking for, and she's been just as reliable ever since."

Jacques nodded. "Anything else?"

"Just that I'll be driving back tomorrow."

Jacques hesitated. "Mmm, I'm not sure that's a good idea," he said. "I've been going through the will and the papers for the Trust, and there is a property in the ninth that must have been Vallade's but is now owned by the Trust. It's… Just a minute." Jacques put his phone down on the table and grabbed the papers he'd been looking at. He turned through four pages and then stopped. "I've got the details here," he said, picking up his phone. "The property is on boulevard des Anges, Mazargues, number one. The deeds are held by the Trust, and the wording in the will dictates that the property should be…" Jacques referred to the papers in his hands and read, "'kept and maintained as it was left, for the use of artists, and any revenue, whether raised through rents, hire or in kind, should be used to further the work of the Trust in…' And then there are lots of conditions that refer to the primary objectives of the Trust, and so on. But what is interesting about this address is that it's the same address where Madame Fribourg was born."

"That's a connection I wasn't expecting," said Didier, and he drained the last drops of rosé in his glass. "Do we know who might be living there at the moment?"

Jacques shook his head. "No, not amongst these papers. However, the terms of the Trust mean that the Principal Curator at the museum is also a member of the Board that manages the Trust. So, I've been checking out the museum in Finistère. According to their website, they are part of the scheme for free admission on the first Sunday of the month. Tomorrow morning, I want to get in touch with the Curator and the archivist, Carolyne Truchon, who manages the Vallade collection."

"That doesn't necessarily mean that the archivists or the curators will be there, does it?"

"I agree, but they offer free lectures tomorrow as well, so I'm hoping to catch at least one of them at some point during the day."

"Good luck with that. I'll check out this address tomorrow morning and let you know what I find."

"OK, thanks, Didier."

Jacques ended the call and slumped back on the sofa in the snug. The pile of legal documents on the coffee table represented a challenge he was not inclined to take up.

Tomorrow. They can wait until tomorrow. He gathered everything together and shoved it into his bag. Sleep was his only requirement.

sunday, june 9th, 10.12

The Vallade Museum in Finistère was located in the farmhouse that had been in the artist's family for generations. The surrounding land containing the orchards had eventually been sold off to a large corporation that had spent decades acquiring pockets of land as the younger generation had left for easier lives and jobs in the surrounding towns and cities. Jacques glanced through the open full-length windows in the dining area. Lucien was sitting on the ground drawing.

"I'm sure you're going to end up as an artist, architect or something like that." He turned to his laptop and dialled the number for the Vallade Museum displayed on the screen. His call was answered almost immediately.

"I'm Jacques Forêt, and I'm undertaking some research about the life and work of Charles-Marcel Vallade, and I would like to make an appointment to talk to Carolyne Truchon, please." Jacques listened.

"I see. Is there someone else I can talk to?" The line became silent for a few moments. Next, there was a click and a new voice.

"OK, and when did Madame Truchon leave?" Jacques jotted down *April 26th – Last Work Day* and underlined it.

"Do you know where she's working now?" A muffled conversation followed before he was informed that no one knew where she currently worked. Jacques thought about asking for Madame Truchon's home address, but realised instantly that her former employer would not give that out over the phone.

"Is there someone else that I could talk to? Perhaps whoever has taken on her role at the moment... Louis Richard," Jacques repeated as he noted the name.

"If I call him about this time tomorrow, will he be available... OK, and it will be a video call as I'm resident in Mende... OK, thank you."

He ended the call. Immediately his mind was whirling in all directions.

"Madame Truchon would be salaried," he muttered. *She would need to give notice, probably three months' notice.* He consulted the calendar on his phone. "That means she would have given her letter of resignation to the Curator on February first, and the three months notice period would have ended on April thirtieth. The day before the Vallade painting was first reported missing." *Coincidence or planned?*

"Groundless speculation," he told himself. But that didn't stop him from viewing the part of the museum website dedicated to personnel, where he found a picture of Carolyne Truchon with a Vallade seascape in the background. Carolyne was listed as the 'Senior Curator for Oils', with Louis Richard as her assistant. He quickly read her curriculum vitae. *Impressive.*

Further down the page on the museum website was a link to a series of ten short video lectures that Carolyne had given over the last two years. He clicked on the link for *Portrait in Black and White* and listened to the content. It was an interesting assessment of the picture, but it didn't tell him anything he hadn't already read in the Simmonet catalogue. In fact, quite a lot of the content seemed to be familiar.

Clicking out of the website, he decided to undertake a general search on the internet for Carolyne Truchon. This brought up more references across various social media sites and Madame Truchon's business page. He clicked on the business page first in the hope that he might get some more personal details. Everything was consistent with her listing for the museum, with the added facts that she was from Quimper and that Châteaulin was listed as her current place of residence. *That might be useful.*

mazargues, sunday, june 9th, 10.52

Didier arrived at the house at the top of boulevard des Anges. He'd had to approach it from another street that appeared to cut off access to the boulevard altogether. But having left a hire car parked by the church, he walked down chemin de Morgiou and discovered a narrow set of steps leading to a short walkway, which in turn led to the boulevard. The property was on his left a little further down, where the street widened out. As he gazed down the length of the twin sets of *platanes*, he noticed the tiredness of the place. It also seemed unnervingly quiet for a city location, almost as if the area had been forgotten.

The house, all on one level, looked to be from the 1930s in style. It was set in the centre of a plot of carefully-tended garden, and the gable-end abutted the high wall that skirted the chemin de Morigou. Didier opened the gate and took the path to the front door. After pressing the bell, he examined the stained-glass panel inset in the top half of the door. The colours were muted, and the semi-abstract nature of the floral design convinced him that the house must be around a hundred years old.

As he was about to leave, he saw a shadow behind the glass and tapped lightly on the wood surround. The figure approached, and the door was pulled open.

"Monsieur?" The woman was in her fifties, Didier supposed. She was petite with dark hair that was liberally interspersed with grey.

"Madame, I'm Didier Duclos," he said. "And I'm undertaking some research into my wife's family tree. She had a relative who once lived at this address. Well, I'm here in Marseille for work for a few days, and I wondered if you could answer a few questions for me."

The woman took a step back. Her look was penetrating. "You're obviously not a tourist," she said. "I suppose I should be grateful for that."

"Tourists, Madame?"

"This house used to belong to the artist Charles-Marcel Vallade. Tourists think they can turn up wherever they want. July and August are the worst months." Didier waited as she studied his face. Smiling, she pulled the door open wide. "Come in," she said, leading him through the hallway and into the *salon*. "You're lucky to find me here. I only got back from painting a mural in Toulouse two days ago, and I'm leaving at the end of next week for a painting course that I run in Greece for the rest of the summer."

Didier smiled as he rounded the threshold corner into the next room, and froze on the spot. The woman moved towards the fireplace, stopped and turned.

"Monsieur Duclos? Is there something the matter?"

Didier recovered his composure and cleared his throat. "No, I'm just surprised to see such a beautiful picture there." He nodded towards the gold-framed oil painting above the fireplace. "One of yours?"

She smiled and turned to look at the artwork. "Stunning, isn't it? And no, it's not one of mine, unfortunately. But I love it." She moved across the room and picked up a small square-framed picture of bright red poppies from the windowsill. "This is one of mine," she said as she handed it to her guest.

Didier nodded. "My wife would love this," he said, noting the cartouche in the bottom left-hand corner containing the signature. "I don't suppose you have another one?"

She smiled. "You can find those anywhere in homeware or art shops. It brings in a regular payment along with the artwork I create for a card company, the occasional work from the museum, and a few other regular requests that help provide some sort of basic and semi-regular salary. The big commissions I get from time to time are for my pension."

She replaced the picture. "Please sit." She took a seat in

an armchair to Didier's right. "I'm a professional artist, Monsieur Duclos. It's part of the terms and conditions for living here."

"Have you lived here long?"

"Almost ten years, and I've enjoyed being here. It's a bit like being in a museum at times, but I love living with the idea that Vallade stood at that window or sat on the garden bench. Well, I hope you understand what I'm trying to say."

"Yes, I think I do, Madame."

"It's Madeleine. Madeleine d'Amencourt."

Didier smiled as he mentally stored the name in his memory. *I think I need to keep my notebook out of sight.*

"My wife's ancestor was living here in the thirties and forties, I believe, but then she seems to disappear from all the records."

"I see. Well, that's quite a bit before my time, but Vallade would have been here back then."

"Actually in this house?" Didier glanced around the room in what he hoped would look like awe-struck respect.

"Not so much in the thirties. I'm told that he kept this little house for his models whilst he and his wife lived in the larger property further down the street. Later, when he returned from America, he sold the other house and moved here. But that was in the late fifties, I think."

"Ah."

"Is it possible your wife's ancestor might have been one of his models?"

"I hope not," said Didier with a level of starchiness that surprised him. "Where models are concerned, artists have an unsavoury reputation."

Madame d'Amencourt grinned and nodded. "Not all of us, Monsieur Duclos, but Vallade was no angel. That much is true. There's a museum dedicated to him and his work in Brittany." She frowned. "Have you thought about approaching them? They have archives full of his papers and letters, you know. If your wife's ancestor disappears from records, there might be a specific reason for that."

"A child, you mean?"

She nodded. "There might be some clues in some of his letters. It wasn't unusual back then for women to move to another area and use a different name."

"You're right, of course. I doubt my wife will be happy with that idea." He paused for a moment. "You said that this house belonged to Vallade, and that working as an artist was a condition of living here. Do you know the reason for that?"

"You'd need to ask the Vallade Trust for the full details, but my understanding was that whoever rented this place had to be an aspiring or emerging artist who would use their time here to extend their portfolio and to improve their technique." She frowned. "I'm not sure now that those were the exact words used, but it's what they meant."

"And you pay rent?"

She nodded. "That's to cover basic costs. Anything over that, the Trust retains for its work."

"Almost ten years is a long time to take advantage of this kind of opportunity."

"Which is why I'm taking as many commissions as possible now. I'm sure I won't get a second extension on my time here."

Didier's gaze moved around the room, taking in the Art Nouveau sconces on the walls, the matching chandelier in the centre of the ceiling, and the period furniture. "It's a beautiful place," he said. "I imagine it will be quite difficult to find somewhere as calm and inspiring as this."

"Yes, and there's the studio space that goes with it, too. That will be a great loss if, and when, I have to move on."

Didier had to stop himself from jumping on her last words. *Jacques never mentioned studio space.* He just smiled and waited in the hope that she would say more.

"And the other house owned by Vallade?"

"No, that was demolished some time ago. It's where my studio is. Whoever has the house has the use of one of the first-floor business units in the small building on the right, about four hundred metres down from here."

"Well, I must err... I've taken up too much of your time

already." Didier took out his phone. "Would you mind if I took a couple of photos, just to show my wife when I get back?"

She grinned. "A phone is nothing compared with the tripods and equipment I sometimes have to put up with."

She got up and stepped into the vestibule. Once alone, Didier quickly captured a copy of the large painting over the fireplace and the small picture of the poppies, then followed her out into the small hallway.

"Thank you, and best of luck with your summer school." He turned and walked back along the path.

Out on the street, the sun's heat burnt heavily through the thinning hair of his scalp. He ducked under the canopy of one of the many trees along the length of the boulevard. Turning to look over the fence surrounding the property, he took a couple of shots of the garden.

"The studio has to be somewhere about there," he said as he scanned the perfectly straight street. Setting off in a direction that took him further away from his car, he checked out the other properties on the right. About halfway down, he spotted a modern low-rise building.

Moving into the small car park, he checked out the entrance. The buzzer operating the door lock had various names for each of the six units. When he looked more closely, there was no name for Unit B1. He pressed the button and, as expected, got no reply. He tried another one.

"Yes?" The irritation in the voice was unmistakable.

"Delivery for d'Amencourt."

"Tut! Number one. House at the top of the street."

Didier grinned. The needed confirmation had been too easy to obtain.

sunday, june 9th, 11.42

Madame Sorina Roşu had dressed carefully that morning, another trip to the local police station dictating her choice of dress, headscarf and jacket. She looked at herself in the mirror in her room.

"Ah! Sorina, why are you making such a bother? It's just an apology," she muttered as she turned herself first left and then right. "And you've delivered plenty of those in your time." *Just not to a policeman before*. The thought caused her stomach to flip.

"*Mama*, come on, we can't be late for lunch," shouted her daughter from somewhere else in the apartment in the ninth *arrondissement*.

"Yes, alright, I'm coming." Sorina bent down to pick up her basket from the floor beside her dressing table. "Do I need that today?" No, she decided as she reached in and took out a small embroidered purse. Taking a deep breath, she pulled her jacket straight and left her room.

The car journey to the local police station with her daughter and son-in-law was quiet, allowing Sorina time to rehearse her French. The couple of sentences Elena had written out for her were already etched into her memory. But extra repetitions would mean that she could dispense with the piece of paper in her hands.

Elena took her mother's arm as they mounted the steps into the station. At the desk was a tall *gendarme* that they had not seen before.

"That's not the right one," said Sorina.

"Yes, *Mama*, I know," she replied in their shared first language. "But when I've explained why we are here, I'm sure we'll be able to talk to the *gendarme* we met last week." Elena smiled. "It'll be alright, *Mama*." Sorina felt her daughter's comforting squeeze on her arm, and listened as Elena switched languages and began speaking in French. Madame Roşu was always amazed at her daughter's command of the foreign tongue. Not that she understood a word of what was being said. The *gendarme* then replied and picked up his phone.

"We need to wait a few moments, *Mama*," Elena said as she moved to sit on a small bench by the wall.

Sorina made herself comfortable. After a moment, she felt in her jacket pocket and pulled out the crumpled piece of paper. As she waited, she kept rehearsing what she had to say.

A few moments later, the officer on the desk was standing in front of them, speaking far too fast and far too French for her ears and mind to cope with.

"The *gendarme* we were speaking to previously is now on holiday, *Mama*. This officer says we can return on Tuesday when he's back at work, or we can leave a message. He says that whatever you have to say, he will write it down and pass it on to his colleague as soon as he's back next week. What do you want to do?"

Sorina was tempted to say that she would rather come back. *But that's a coward's way out.* "We're here, Elena. We'll do this now, and that will be the end of it."

Elena smiled. Turning to the desk officer, she translated her mother's words.

With a flounce of ceremony, the officer returned to his post behind the desk, picked up a statement sheet and a pen and stood poised to record Sorina's words.

"I have now heard from my employer, Madame Apollinaire," said Sorina in her heavily accented French. She looked at the piece of paper in her hands. "I thought something bad had happened to her, but she has been away working. I am sorry to have caus…" She faltered on the word, and Elena whispered it instantly. "Caused any unnecessary work. Thank you." Sorina took a gulp of air and turned to her daughter, who smiled.

"Just sign the form, *Mama*, and then we can go and meet

the others at the restaurant."

Sorina took the offered pen and signed as required. Out in the sunshine, she felt as though a heavy weight had been lifted from her shoulders. With a lightness of step that had eluded her earlier, she walked to the car and got in.

marseille, sunday, june 9th, 14.18

In the cabin on his hired boat, Didier logged on to his laptop and video-called Jacques. It was a few moments before his colleague picked up the call and appeared on the screen.

"Hang on Didier," said Jacques. "I've got war in the snug. I'll be back in a moment."

Didier grinned. As he waited, he could hear Jacques in the background. His tone was thunderous as he told his guests that fighting was not acceptable behaviour. Next came the imposed sitting in silence. Lucien was banished to one chair, and his friend Charles dismissed to another.

Jacques resumed his seat and rolled his eyes. "Sorry about that."

"Don't worry, Jacques, my two sons were regularly at war! He'll grow out of it."

"They have to remain quiet for the next ten minutes, or Charles goes home," said Jacques as he set the alarm on his phone. "I've got a few moments now, or we can re-schedule."

"It's OK, but I think we need more than ten minutes."

"Alright. So, the visit to the house on boulevard des Anges, how did that go?"

"More interesting than I expected it to be," said Didier. "The present occupant is Madeleine d'Amencourt, a single woman in her fifties who is a professional artist. She rents the property from the Trust and has been there for almost ten years."

"Just a minute," said Jacques. Didier heard him scrabbling through his papers. "Here it is. The conditions of use of that property are for a maximum of five years. So, why is she still there?"

"Apparently her lease was extended by the Trust. But,

from what she told me, I would describe her as an established artist rather than an aspiring or emerging one. Her words, not mine."

Jacques flicked over a page. "That's what it says here. Again, why is she still there?"

"Since I got back to the boat, I've been doing a bit of research and—" A squeal of laughter came from somewhere in Jacques' chalet, and he disappeared from the screen.

Didier waited. In the background, he couldn't hear what was being said, but he recognised the severe tone in Jacques' voice. Then there was a moment of silence, followed by a tumultuous shout of "Outside!" from the children.

"We're moving," said Jacques as he re-appeared on screen. Didier chuckled to himself and cast his mind back to when his boys were the same age. In the intervening moments, he got himself a beer from the small fridge. The afternoon heat was beginning to get oppressive. Taking his cue from Jacques and the children, he decided to move out into the fresh air. With the deck partially enclosed as it was, he would be in the shade and still get the benefit from the breeze floating into the harbour from the sea.

"Play nicely," said Jacques as he sat down again. "Where were we?"

Didier glanced at the screen and realised Jacques must be on the chalet porch. In the background, he could hear the boys playing happily.

"Madame d'Amencourt," said Didier. "When I got back here, I did a bit of research on her. She has shown her artwork at several exhibitions. She also has a website on which she accepts commissions and sells her work direct to the customer. I've already sent you the link, but I suppose you've been too busy to get to that yet."

Jacques nodded. "Those two have a very up-and-down friendship. One minute happy and quiet, and the next fighting."

Didier smiled. "As we were chatting, Madame d'Amencourt mentioned that she did some work for the museum. She didn't name it, but I took her to mean the Vallade Museum, and, therefore, the Trust."

"Interesting," said Jacques. "Were you able to find out what kind of work?"

"I had gone there on an invented pretext, Jacques. The way the conversation was progressing, if I'd asked for specifics, it might have derailed things."

"OK. Did you pick up anything else?"

Didier nodded. "I managed to get some photos of the house and some artwork in there." He held his phone up to his screen for Jacques to see.

"That's 'Sunday Afternoon on the Beach'."

"I know. And I didn't get the chance to look to see if it was genuine or not."

"How many copies of this painting are there?"

Didier shrugged. "Have you spoken to the archivist at the museum yet?"

"No, but I have a video call with Louis Richard, one of the senior curators, tomorrow morning. I'll ask about the work done by Madame d'Amencourt and these multiple copies of 'Sunday Afternoon'."

"The last, and perhaps the most significant, thing is the signature she uses on her artwork." Didier turned to his phone, swiped the screen, and then enlarged and centred the detail from the picture of the poppies. "Just take a look at that cartouche."

Jacques moved closer to the screen and stared. "That's the forger's mark turned through ninety degrees to the right."

Didier nodded. "Yes, it is. I've also sent you that photo so you can compare it with those from Madame Fribourg's picture." There was a deep frown on Didier's face.

"What is it?"

"Madame d'Amencourt didn't come across to me as a forger, Jacques. She didn't seem to me to be any kind of criminal."

Jacques sat back in his chair. "Alright. Let's look at what we have. What motive does she have?"

"I can only see money. A need for money or more of it. She intimated that she may be homeless once her tenure at the Vallade house reaches ten years."

"Money can be a great motivator," agreed Jacques. "But what about the means?"

Didier took a drink of his beer. "She personally has the means to create the forgery, and she has the talent. But accessing the gallery or the museum to obtain the original or blackmailing the courier, I don't think so. This crime took a lot of planning. If she did mastermind the theft, I'd be stunned. And if she didn't, then there must be others involved."

"Which makes me wonder, Didier, if she may have been an unwitting forger. You said she had done some work for the museum. What if that work was creating a copy to replace the original?"

"But what does she do with the originals?"

Jacques let out a sigh. "This case has been frustrating from the very start. But if she is an unwitting forger, then the copy and the original must both go back to whoever is really behind this."

"Mm. And what's your take on opportunity?"

"That it brings further frustration, damn it! Madame Fribourg said she has always refused requests from the Trust for her picture to be included in special exhibitions."

"Wait a minute, Jacques. Are you suggesting that the Trust could quite easily have switched the paintings themselves?"

"It's possible, but if so, what was their motivation? It comes back to the point I made the other day. Why steal something that you already have access to and half-own? And how would any one individual get away with that? The Trust has numerous highly qualified staff. Any fakes would be spotted immediately."

Loud, boisterous squeals made Didier jump. Jacques got up and disappeared from the screen.

"Charles, what are you doing up there? Lucien, do not move. Neither of you move AT ALL."

Didier couldn't see what was happening but could make an educated guess. The dregs of his beer were warm. He got up to fetch another one and refreshed his glass.

The drama in Messandrierre seemed to be continuing. The sun was getting hotter, and Didier wanted some time to himself. A quarter of the way down his beer, he decided it was time to quit the video call. He typed out a message in the chat function.

> Hope all OK your end. Staying here tonight. If you need me to follow up on anything here – text/email. Be back <u>tomorrow</u> around <u>14.00</u>.

messandrierre, sunday, june 9th, 20.48

Jacques stared into the glass of whisky in his hand, debating when and how Madame Fribourg's artwork had been exchanged. Whichever way he looked at it, the switch had to have taken place either at the gallery in Mende or the museum in Finistère. *But how?* The question seemed to be forever circling in his mind.

A contented snort through the baby monitor broke Jacques' chain of thoughts. He glanced at his watch.

"I'm not surprised at that," he said as he got up and dashed up the stairs to Lucien's room. His son was fast asleep. The bedtime story and the bookmark had slipped onto the floor, and the duvet was askew. Jacques tiptoed in and straightened the cover, picked up the book, marked the page and placed it back on the shelf. At the threshold, he stopped and looked at the small boy in a bed that seemed to engulf him.

"It's been a pretty exhausting day for both of us," he whispered. A dark, menacing thought clouded his mind. He switched off the light and pulled the door until it was almost closed. At the top of the stairs, he grabbed the metal newel post, his grip so tight his knuckles were white. *That won't happen.*

"That won't happen," he said. "Audrey Taillard will win and I WILL be doing this every night for as long as Lucien needs me to." He glanced out of the loft window. Clouds were shifting across the darkening sky as the slight wind ruffled through the branches of the trees. In the distance, the mountain ridge remained steadfast. Jacques let go of the post and quietly went back to the snug.

Closing the door behind him, he caught sight of the four volumes of the Vallade catalogue. He sat down and picked out the second volume. The book on portraiture was organised in the same way as the first, with chapters using the same headings where relevant. Jacques turned to a section entitled *The Brittany Years: 1911-1937*, where he had last stopped. He began reading and making notes.

The artworks were not as interesting to him as the seascapes and landscapes had been. But he persevered. He wanted to be armed with as much knowledge as could possibly be gleaned from Professor Simmonet's study, in preparation for his discussion with the museum curator the following morning.

The earlier portraits included some of Vallade's wife and his only son. He mostly just glanced at the notes accompanying each one. But he stopped and studied picture *P24, Mother and Child*, completed in 1927. A head-and-shoulders study of his wife holding her son. He blinked back a tear as he recalled a similar pose adopted by Beth and Lucien just before the accident. He pulled his thumb and forefinger across his eyes and squeezed the bridge of his nose tight. *That photograph is in—* He wouldn't let himself complete the thought.

Turning the page, he continued reading. There were only one or two other portraits of the artist's family. The following chapter – *The American Years: 1938-1946* – was much more absorbing. Jacques found himself debating some of Simmonet's contentions about the political nature of the work.

The last chapter provided Jacques with the most relevant notes for his case, and the portrait, *P157 Madame Apollinaire*, stopped him dead. He stared at the face of the woman. Something that he had seen somewhere before jumped out from the picture. He turned back to the opening paragraphs and the, now always expected, excerpt from a letter. A realisation that had been snatching at the fringe of his subconscious deployed as a conscious thought. He flipped back to the page containing *Mother and Child*, then forward to *Madame Apollinaire*, and finally back to the introduction to that section of the book.

Jacques grabbed his phone and sent a text to Didier.

> How many people do you know with pale green eyes?

The reply was almost instantaneous.

> Just the one. Madame Fribourg

> Am visiting Mme F <u>tomorrow</u>. Can you stay & watch Mme d'Amencourt?

> Won't be easy – she knows me. Street is quiet and narrow. Can set up a camera I think.

> OK. Do that asap please. Thanks.

THE FINAL YEARS: 1947-1972

> *My mother was always my fiercest critic – my Apollinaire – and, when I married, I hoped my wife would fulfil that role. But her values were different from mine, as demonstrated later...*
>
> *I couldn't believe my luck on my return to France when a new face – une ingénue – walked into my studio. She soon became my confidante, my critic, my new Apollinaire...*
>
> —Charles-Marcel Vallade, 1968

The grief, the loneliness, the episodes of despair that Vallade experienced in America crossed the ocean with him when he first returned to France.

His output in the first two years after his return was of poor quality, lacking in direction and more akin to the work of an untrained amateur.

The acrimonious divorce had made him realise that he needed to provide for the future – his own in the immediate term, and his work in the long term. The first germ of an idea for what would become the Vallade Museum and Trust was sown.

His artistic talent was prompted into being once again after he moved back to Mazargues. The landscape, the coast, the light, *'set his mind free'* he told me some years later. Perhaps that was how he chose to see it. Having examined his work in depth over many years, I am of the opinion that his first and most stunning work, his catalyst for continuing to paint until his death in 1972, was **P173 *Madame Apollinaire.***

I go into much more detail about the artwork in my accompanying notes. But here, in this short introductory chapter, it is enough for me to say that his use of light on the face and shoulders of the subject is exemplary. He created many works following this, but none with the extraordinary cast, brilliance of colour or perspective of *Madame Apollinaire*.

mende, monday, june 10th, 10.02

Jacques' desk was covered in papers and books, all of which related to Vallade. At the side of his laptop was a set of initial questions. The answers he received from the archivist at the Vallade Museum would prompt other queries, he was sure, but he could handle that. Finally ready, Jacques made the call. On the second ring, it was picked up by Monsieur Louis Richard. The archivist, a greyed-haired man who looked to be in his fifties, removed his spectacles and smiled.

"*Bonjour*, Monsieur Forêt," he said.

"Monsieur Richard, *bonjour* and thank you for making time available to speak to me. I would like to talk about Vallade, his work, his life, and a little bit about the museum and Trust, too."

Louis Richard nodded.

"But first, perhaps I can ask a few questions about you and your post at the museum."

Again Monsieur Richard nodded his agreement.

"How long have you been with the Trust?"

"Almost thirty years, now."

"And I believe you are an art historian?"

"Yes, but I'm also one of the conservators."

I am going to have to tease every morsel of information out of you, I think. Jacques made a note of the additional role on his crib sheet.

"And to what extent do you get involved in the day-to-day work of the museum?"

"Across the board, really. Since Carolyne left, I'm now responsible for overseeing anything in connection with Vallade's oil paintings, whether they are on canvas or panel. So, any re-arrangements of the current displays will be down to me. Any requests for loans will come to me, and any special exhibitions we want to run will be within my remit."

Now that's much better, Monsieur Richard. Let's hope this openness continues.

"You mentioned Carolyne. Is that Carolyne Truchon?"

"Yes, my previous boss. She resigned at the end of last month."

As Jacques glanced at the screen, he thought he saw a glimmer of a gleam in the archivist's eyes as he said that. *Interesting.*

"Will that mean a promotion for you?"

"I hope so. Don't misunderstand me, Monsieur Forêt—"

"Jacques, please, Monsieur Richard."

"And it's Louis for me," he said with a bright smile on his face. "Yes, where was I? Oh, of course, Carolyne. She is an excellent curator, and she knows her subject inside out, but, erm, Carolyne was very much in charge when she was here. She hardly ever delegated, and when she went on leave, she made sure there was virtually nothing for me to do. She even postponed her monthly meetings rather than continuing them and letting me chair and manage the business," he added, a look of disapproval on his face.

"I can see how frustrating that would be, and I've known a few bosses myself who work like that. You must be relieved to be given a free hand at last."

"I am, and I hope I might be successful in the recruitment exercise for her replacement."

Jacques smiled. "So, you've been with the Trust for about thirty years. That means that you must have come across Professor Gabriel Simmonet."

"Yes, he was Chairman of the Board when I was first recruited after leaving university in 1989. An extremely clever man. He was on my recruitment panel, you know. I also had the pleasure of helping him with the archive of letters and papers that Vallade left us."

"In what way?"

"Searching things out in the archive for him. General

research at other times, and sometimes social history research, too. You'll see my name if you look at the acknowledgements at the back of his catalogue on Vallade. I know it's one among many, but it is still there." The bristle of triumph that swept across the archivist's face was not lost on Jacques.

"I've been asked to find a particular painting, and it appears there are numerous copies. I'm aware that some might be authorised copies, but I'm an ex-policeman, Louis, so I understand that the art world is attractive to forgers. How do you differentiate between the real works, the copies and the fakes?"

"It's very difficult," Louis replied. "And the task is further complicated when you have an artist who not only paints a scene more than once but also uses the same title for all the various versions. Now, Vallade was not alone in doing that – so did Sisley, Monet, and many others. But the short answer to your question is the provenance. By that I mean the painting's actual commercial, public or private history."

"What about 'Sunday Afternoon on the Beach'? Can you be definitive about the versions of that?"

"Yes, and Simmonet's catalogue does detail only some of this. The version completed in 1921 is in private ownership – it was the subject of a lawsuit after Vallade died, and was settled out of court. That oil on canvas was created from a panel that Vallade had roughed out, also in oils, two years before. He then went on to use that panel for other versions of the scene, and there are slight differences in each re-creation. There are also a couple of watercolours that were probably based on the panel or possibly just created from memory. We will never be sure of that unless some new evidence comes to light. In our collection, we have the rough panel, two oil versions of the scene, and the watercolours. We are certain our holdings are genuine. We know the original oil in private ownership is also genuine. We have access to that painting, which joins our display for six months each year."

Not genuine any more, thought Jacques. "The cache of letters and papers, Louis, might it be possible to identify the actual subjects in Vallade's paintings?"

Louis thought for a moment. "That would depend on who you mean. There is some correspondence where Vallade makes passing references to subjects in his work. Some of our information has come from research. As an example, we've used historical data from voters' lists and census records. Vallade may have written that a person in a picture is the family cook. From the date, we can check who was in the household at that time and make an assumption. But it's not as precise as you might think or hope."

"What about his muses? Is that the right word?"

Louis grinned. "Ah yes, muse if you wish. To us, they are models who appear across the whole body of his work. There were a few of those over the years."

"So, can you identify the model in his painting 'Madame Apollinaire'?"

"Which one?"

Jacques stared at the screen. *Not more multiple copies.* "The oil painting I'm interested in was completed on his return to France after 1947."

"Ah yes, that one. A fabulous piece of work. We believe the woman in that picture is Alexandrine Chapron. But the —"

"Are you sure about that?" That was a name he hadn't expected.

"Oh yes," said Louis. "Alexandrine Chapron is named in Vallade's will."

Jacques nodded. He'd come across that little nugget of information when he'd applied the toothcomb of his mind to the document on Saturday. Another piece of critical information that his client, Madame Fribourg, had kept to herself. When he'd considered her reasons for doing so, he'd concluded that the possibilities were numerous. The most likely ones at the top of his list were shame or possible manipulation.

"I was aware of that, Louis, but I was hoping for

something pre-dating the will. Some correspondence, perhaps."

"With Alexandrine?"

"Not necessarily."

Louis frowned. "I can't be certain without checking the archives, but I believe there may be something in the cache of papers we inherited from Professor Simmonet. What I am certain about is that Alexandrine lived with Vallade right up until his death. From the fifties to the sixties, we believe they were in a relationship, but Vallade still had his own house and studio where he spent most of his time. Alexandrine had a daughter, and it was when she left home in 1968 that Vallade sold his own property and moved in with Madame Chapron."

"Would it be possible to search out that evidence?"

"Oh yes. I can do that for you quite easily. We've been gradually digitising our archive, and I can email you what we have."

"Thank you. Before I interrupted you, you were talking about 'Madame Apollinaire' and the other versions."

"Yes, I was. The earlier 'Madame Apollinaire' versions are of his mother. We have a watercolour and a later panel in oil. Both have a similar pose and facial profile to the Alexandrine Chapron painting."

"OK. Thank you," said Jacques. *So, the Simmonet Catalogue is not quite as complete and comprehensive as I thought.* "Just a few more questions. 'Sunday Afternoon on the Beach', when the picture arrives for its six-months display, do you undertake any checks for authenticity?"

"Oh yes, we are rigorous in handling artworks coming in and going out on loan. We use a specialist carrier, and each picture leaves us fully packaged, protected, and sealed. The carrier covers our packaging with their own, which is also sealed, and the travel is constantly tracked. Everything is signed in and out at every stage, and there are always two signatures. There's no room for error."

That's what I thought. This means there is only one other possibility. "Going back to Carolyne, I would still like to talk to her. Do you know where she's working now?"

"No, I don't. Carolyne never said anything about her new post. I assumed she had a job lined up for later in the year as she said she was going to go away for a while."

"Did she say where her holiday would be?"

Louis frowned. "Not that I can recall, but I think we did get a postcard from her which came from Nîmes, I think, or somewhere down that end of the country. But she lives in Châteaulin and has an answerphone on her landline. You could leave a message for her for when she gets back."

"Thanks, but I need to speak to her quite urgently. Does she have a mobile number?"

"Yes, and I can let you have that as well," he said as he reached for his phone and scrolled through his contact list. Jacques jotted down the landline and mobile numbers as Louis read them out.

"Thanks, Louis, that's very helpful. I have just one other thing I want to discuss with you. A Madame Madeleine d'Amencourt is renting the Vallade property in Mazargues. Do you know anything about that?"

"I do now," he said, his disapproval apparent on his face. "The Trust maintains that property for the use of young artists to enable them to develop their talent. I had no idea that Carolyne had agreed with the Board of Trustees that Madame d'Amencourt could remain there for as long as she has. I wasn't even aware that managing that was part of Carolyne's, and now my, job until a couple of weeks ago, when the Secretary to the Board told me the current tenure will expire in three months' time." Louis paused for breath.

"So what will happen now?"

"I've checked all the rules, Jacques, and from now on we are going to manage that property how it was intended to be managed. I was so surprised that Carolyne had let this situation continue for so long. I spoke to Madame d'Amencourt late on Friday afternoon to let her know that we won't be continuing the special arrangement that she had with Carolyne. She will be given formal notice to quit in the next couple of days."

"If the use of that property has been mismanaged, what do you think the Trust will do about it?"

"It's already been decided, Jacques. There will be an internal enquiry." Louis instantly became tight-lipped as he stared at Jacques.

An internal enquiry will bring recommendations, thought Jacques. *And recommendations might mean legal action against Carolyne Truchon. Interesting.*

Jacques nodded. "Thank you, Louis, you've been very helpful. May I call you if I have any further questions?"

"Of course, and I hope you will be able to visit us in the near future."

"I think my son would like that."

Jacques clicked out of the video call, pushed his chair back to the wall and considered his next move. *Do I go after Carolyne Truchon or Madame d'Amencourt?* With no direct evidence that Carolyne had done anything other than leave her job and take some time for herself, he wondered if he really had any reason to go after her.

"It's the timing that makes me suspicious. In addition, we have only one other avenue to pursue," he said. He turned his thoughts to Madame d'Amencourt, the apparent creator of Madame Fribourg's forgery. Didier's words echoed through his mind: *She didn't seem to me to be any kind of criminal.*

He made a decision and grabbed his phone. He dialled Carolyne's mobile number and got the message it hadn't been possible to connect the call. He dialled again and got the same message. Trying the landline next, the call just disconnected as though the number had been discontinued. He tried a second time to be sure.

"And that's even more interesting,' he said, just as Maxim came into his room.

"Sorry, Jacques, but there's a woman in the foyer. She only wants to speak to you. She says she wants you to find a painting that is hers."

"Let me guess," said Jacques as he got up and pulled his jacket off the back of the chair. "It's 'Sunday Afternoon on the Beach'."

"Yes," said Maxim. "How did you know?"

"I didn't. It's just that there seem to be so many versions of this painting that it wouldn't surprise me if there was yet another," he said as he collected the plans for the gallery. "I need to see Madame Fribourg. Can you go and talk to the lady in the foyer, please? Get her full details and her story about the painting, explain that I'm not available, and we'll catch up when I get back." Jacques raced out of the room and down the stairs.

monday, june 10th, 11.18

At the shop and gallery on rue du Soubeyran, a couple of women were perusing the cards as Jacques walked in.

"*Bonjour, Mesdames*," he said as he entered. He turned immediately to the counter. "Is Madame Fribourg here?"

The assistant behind the counter, a different one from his previous visits, pointed to the small office.

"In there," she said. Jacques stepped past the customers and moved to the rear of the space. He tapped on the door marked *Privé*.

"*Entrez*," came a voice from behind the door.

Jacques opened the door and stood on the threshold. "Madame Fribourg, I want to check out one of my theories, and I will need your help as my colleague is not available today."

"Of course. What can I do?"

Standing aside but keeping the door open, he said, "If we could go to the top floor, please?"

Madame Fribourg got up and led the way up the stairs. Jacques stopped as he reached the top of the steps on the third floor and looked at the room. It was just as he remembered it. A long rectangle with white panels on the wall space between the windows, the white vertical blinds for each one closed against the bright sunshine. He knelt on one knee, placed the room plan on the floor and added some small weights to keep the rolled sheet flat.

"This is my dilemma, Madame. The plan shows a fire exit in that wall at the back, over to our left."

Madame Fribourg nodded. "And it is still there."

"But how is it accessed? Because fire regulations state that the exit must be available to use in an emergency."

"It can be. Those two panels can be opened."

"Without removing the artwork?"

"Yes, that's why we can't hang large oils with heavy frames on that part of the wall."

Jacques looked at the display. Three watercolours to the left and two small panels to the right. "And what's behind the wall panels?"

"Just a standard fire exit, as far as I can remember."

"Can you show me how to open them, please?"

"Yes, but I will need help." She went to the back wall. "The panel has runners inset underneath, and the hinges are on the right. The catches are here on the left." She bent down to spring a catch at the bottom and another one at the centre. "I'm not tall enough to reach the top one. So our emergency procedure shows that if we need to use this exit, Henriette will come up here and open it."

Jacques looked down at her. "Of course," he said as he reached for the final catch and opened it. He pulled the panel away from the wall. It was surprisingly light and easy to do. Turning back to the space behind, he examined the floor. The accumulated dust motes in the recess along the panel length indicated that it hadn't been moved for quite a while.

"When did you last run a fire drill, Madame?"

Jacques could see a slight colouration rising on Madame Fribourg's cheeks. "Last November," she said quietly.

"I expect your fire certificate will be due for renewal in December or January?"

Madame Fribourg nodded. "December," she said.

Jacques turned his attention to the standard fire exit door behind. As he examined the space and the door, he was satisfied that no one had used it recently.

"OK," he said. "I've seen everything I need to see here."

Next, he looked up at the ceiling. The old beams were still visible and intact. But the space between them had been boarded, plastered and painted. There was no sign of access to the roof area.

"Is there any way into the roof space from this room?"

"No. We used to have access to the roof from here, but as

part of the insurance from the museum, we had to have that sealed. The roof space above here is connected with the properties on our right. When the renovations were undertaken here, that access was also sealed."

"Thank you. That leaves us with only one possibility," Jacques muttered, as he glanced around the room for the last time.

"What do you mean, Monsieur?"

"I think I know who is behind the theft of your painting."

Madame Fribourg waited. Jacques wandered around the room, gazing at the exhibits.

"This collection, Madame, do you own every one of them?"

"Yes. Most came from my mother, who inherited them. Some I've acquired myself. For instance, I found these two watercolours at a *vide-grenier* in Chaumont. They didn't cost that much, and the seller didn't know what he had. The panels here in the centre were inherited. My husband and I bought the two oils over there at auction when Vallade wasn't selling well."

"I know you said that you have never loaned out 'Sunday Afternoon on the Beach'. But what about these others?"

"No, never."

"There's something I'm missing. What am I not seeing?" Jacques put his hands on his hips and stared at the floor.

"Conservation, Madame Fribourg," he said, whipping his head upright. "Cleaning, conservation, and restoration. How do you do that?"

"I don't. The museum does that for us."

"Do they?" Jacques gathered up the plan and re-rolled it. "Check whichever artworks have been to the museum for cleaning or restoration. I'll be in touch as soon as I can." He bounded down the stairs leaving Madame Fribourg to the task he had just asked her to complete.

Jacques took a left from the gallery and marched along Soubeyran and across the ring road as he made his way to the police station. He hoped that his visit would not be in vain.

At the desk was an officer he didn't recognise.

"Jacques Forêt for *Gendarme* Lefèvre," he said. "He asked me on Saturday to come in and make a statement in connection with a case he has open."

Asked to sit and wait, Jacques paced backwards and forwards across the space. It helped his brain as it circled round and round the same questions and possible answers.

"Come through," said Lefèvre.

Jacques followed his ex-colleague into an interview room and sat down. "I need a favour," he said.

Lefèvre grimaced as he reached for a blank statement form. "You know I can't necessarily agree to that. But tell me what it is anyway."

"Carolyne Truchon, an art historian and museum curator, lives in Châteaulin, and I know that is out of your area. But hear me out. I've been trying to contact her. There's no answer at her home address. I think the line has been disconnected. Her mobile is ringing unobtainable. Either she's deliberately gone to ground, or she's missing. Wherever she is, I believe she will have with her, or have access to, several valuable original works of art which have been stolen."

"That last part puts an interesting spin on your request for a favour," said Lefèvre. "And if the art has been stolen, have the owners notified the police?"

"That's what's so clever about this, Lefèvre. The originals have been replaced with forgeries that have yet to be identified. I'm in contact with a victim of one of the thefts, and I think I know who the forger is. But I don't know the extent to which the forger was involved in the overall plan, nor the precise number of items that have been stolen."

"Do you have a description of Carolyne Truchon?"

"I can do better than that," said Jacques pulling out his notebook. "Check this website, and here are the numbers I've been calling."

Lefèvre pushed the statement form across to Jacques and

took out his own notebook. He quickly copied down the details relating to Carolyne Truchon. "I'm assuming you haven't forgotten how to make a statement."

Jacques grinned. "Of course not."

"Wait there and get writing. I need everything you can remember about that rogue trader." Lefèvre left the room.

Twenty minutes later, with his statement complete, Jacques video-called Didier.

"Didier, I'm in a police interview room. I need to update you. Are you still watching Madame d'Amencourt?"

"Yes. I'm in an Airbnb room in Mazargues. I thought it might be sensible to stay close. I've got a camera rigged under cover of some foliage, and I can see the front door of the property on boulevard des Anges."

"Good. Anything of note?"

"Yes. I think Madame d'Amencourt is planning to make a move. A smartly-dressed man from a removal firm called on her earlier today. He was in there for about an hour, so I'm guessing she's getting ready to leave. She did say she was going to Greece for the summer. So it could all be innocent. As he stood at the front door waiting to be let in, I could clearly see the company's name on the back of his jacket. It was Labalte and Baptiste."

"That's interesting. It's the same removal company used by the Vallade Museum, and suggests that she might be moving some valuables. Anything else, Didier?"

"Not so far."

"I've been trying to track down Carolyne Truchon from the museum. She's resigned from her post and is not answering her landline or mobile. Some interesting information came from my discussion with Louis Richard at the Vallade Museum. Carolyne and Madame d'Amencourt were in contact with each other. Carolyne set up the special arrangement so Madame d'Amencourt could stay at the property in Mazargues."

"Which means they were possibly working together."

"It would appear so. I've ruled out the exchange of the

pictures taking place at the gallery here. It has to be at the Vallade Museum. I've also asked Madame Fribourg to check her other oils to see if they are genuine. I think they may also have been swapped. There's—"

Jacques looked up as Lefèvre entered the room. "Hold on, Didier." He put his phone on the table.

"Sorry to keep you waiting, Jacques. But it's not just theft and forgery," said Lefèvre as he sat down opposite Jacques. "It's also murder." He held up the copy of the mortuary photo he'd downloaded from the computer system. "Marseille police have an unknown female who looks remarkably like your Carolyne Truchon."

Jacques nodded. "When was she killed?"

"May the first," said Lefèvre. "The investigating officer is *Inspecteur* Graves. He wants to talk to you."

Jacques smiled. "May the first. That fits. Did you get that, Didier?"

"Yes, Jacques, thanks."

"I know *Inspecteur* Graves from a previous investigation. I'll call him from my office. And here's your statement about the rogue trader. If he contacts me as he said he would, I'll let you know." Jacques picked up his phone and stood.

"Thanks, Jacques," said Lefèvre.

Out on the street, Jacques spoke to Didier. "How close are you to Madame d'Amencourt's current residence?"

"A ten-minute walk away," he said. "And I'm on my way over there now."

"Good. Be careful, Didier. I'm heading back to the office to talk to Graves." Jacques strode out across town.

mazargues, monday, june 10th, 12.03

Didier hesitated on the porch of number one boulevard des Anges. Before knocking, he needed to recover his breath and get his story straight in his head. He knew he had to make sure she invited him in. He removed his sunglasses and tapped on the door. Madame d'Amencourt's shadow appeared almost immediately behind the glass panel.

"Monsieur Duclos," she said, holding the door wide open. "This is a surprise."

"Yes, and I'm sorry to bother you again, Madame. When I spoke to my wife after my last visit, she had more questions. I was wondering if you could give me a little more of your time to—"

"I'm very busy today." She cut him off with a sharpness of tone that hadn't been displayed when he had called previously.

Didier frowned. "I realise this is an imposition, Madame d'Amencourt, but I will be in a meeting all morning tomorrow and I leave immediately after that. Today is my last opportunity to complete this research for my wife."

She let out a deep sigh. "Very well, come in." She stepped back and closed the door behind her visitor. "In the *salon*," she said. It was more of an order than a request.

"Thank you." As Didier moved round to sit on the sofa, he glanced at the landscape above the fireplace. *Still here.* He settled himself. Madame d'Amencourt took the chair to his right. He smiled at her. "That picture is stunning, isn't it?"

Madame nodded. "Your questions, Monsieur Duclos?"

Now is the moment of truth. "When I was here the other day, it wasn't because I wanted to check out this address for my wife. I was here because I'm a private investigator, and my colleague and I believe you have been instrumental in depriving a charitable organisation, and some private individuals, of their artwork. We also believe that you have not been working alone."

There was a split second before she replied.

"Preposterous," she spat out.

And that moment of hesitation tells me I'm on the right track. Didier took out his phone and showed her the picture of Carolyne Truchon.

"Do you know this woman?"

"No, I've never seen her before." Madame d'Amencourt smiled. "And I don't know what you're talking about. As I said the other day, I am a professional artist. I sometimes undertake work as a copyist. That doesn't make me a criminal, Monsieur Duclos." The sickly-sweet smile crossed her face again.

"It does when the owner – in this case the Vallade Museum and Madame Agnès Fribourg – does not authorise the copies." Didier saw a fleeting change in her expression. "Agnès Fribourg," he repeated. "Have you come across that name before?"

The smile was back. "No, not that I can remember."

"What about Carolyne Truchon? Any recollection of that name?"

Madame d'Amencourt remained tight-lipped and stared ahead.

"What about Monsieur Louis Richard?"

"No."

"That's strange, because Monsieur Richard works at the Vallade Museum. According to my colleague, Monsieur Richard spoke to you on Friday afternoon about your continued residence here."

"Oh, that Louis. Yes, of course. Sorry, I didn't realise you meant him. To me, he's just Louis at the museum."

Didier stared at her. "Louis worked for Carolyne Truchon. So I'm surprised you haven't heard that name. They have been working together all the time you've been living here. It was Carolyne who persuaded the Board at the

Trust to waive the five-year limit on your stay here. A very noble act, wouldn't you say, for someone you say you've never met or even heard of."

"Some people are very generous with their time. I'm not one of them. If you wouldn't mind, Monsieur Duclos." She stood up. "I have plenty of work to do before I leave."

Didier remained where he was. "I was also wondering, Madame d'Amencourt, if you knew that Carolyne is dead. Found murdered a few metres from this property. Because of my colleague's work, we've been able to identify the body for the local police."

Didier watched as she swallowed hard. "We've connected all the dots, Madame. But I do have one genuine question. Why? Why forge the paintings?"

The silence in the room stretched and became oppressive.

"The police are on their way, Madame," Didier said. "My colleague has taken care of that."

"Seven years," she whispered. "I've been working on this for seven years, and then Carolyne comes here and tells me that I can't get my full reward until the paintings are sold. I wasn't having that. That's why I've still got that landscape. When she came here to collect it, I was waiting for her—"

A sharp bang on the front door made them both start. "Police." Another heavy-fisted hit on the back door, and more shouts of "Police" followed.

Justice is about to be done. Didier stood and waited.

mende, monday, june 10th, 14.28

Settling at his desk again, Jacques scanned the whiteboard for messages. A missed call from Madame Taillard, and a note about the woman who had come into the office asking about a painting. Jacques went through to the main office.

"Maxim, the lady who called earlier. What was that about?"

"She said she is the granddaughter of Madame Guiot, whom Charles-Marcel Vallade employed as a model. She currently lives in St Étienne and wants us to find a picture given to her grandmother. The artwork is 'Sunday Afternoon on the Beach'."

Jacques let out a sigh. "Why has she come to us?"

"She saw the note I put on our website to tempt Madame Fribourg to contact us. I've taken it down now."

"Alright. There is no Madame Guiot named in Vallade's will. So, in the absence of any contrary evidence, that painting belongs to Madame Fribourg. The lady will need to consult a lawyer if she wants to make a case about ownership." Jacques got up. "And I don't think I've got the energy for another case about art."

Returning to his desk, he telephoned Audrey Taillard. "Madame Taillard, I've got a message to ring you." He listened as the *avocat* explained that she had rebutted all the evidence and was asking for a dismissal.

"Will that work?" Jacques held his breath as she spoke. Gradually his deep frown lessened, and he took a gulp of air.

"You're sure it will work?" As soon as he said the words, he knew what her answer would be. Nothing within the law was ever certain until it was formally decided. He closed the call as a slow smile spread across his face.

col de la tourette, saturday, june 15th

Jacques parked the bike in the same spot as he had done two weeks before. Today the sun was stronger and more damaging. The previous north-westerly breeze was supplanted by a still and warm pocket of air. Jacques zipped down the front of his leathers and pulled his arms out of the top half of the all-in-one. It was just too hot to be wearing leathers. Even on the bike at full blast on a mountain road.

Leaning against the wooden fence at the back of the *aire de repos*, he checked his watch. *Four minutes and he should be here*. Jacques looked at the switchback junction across the road.

"Everyone set?" He didn't need to ask the question because he already knew the answer. But he asked it anyway. It was contact. The question and the answers that he got were contact. The right kind of contact. The wrong kind was the contact with the man he was meeting. The man for whom he was the decoy.

As a detective in Paris, he'd played this role many times before. He'd never liked the part, but he'd done it. Today he was doing it again. And he still didn't like it.

The sun, hot on the back of his favourite white shirt, was beginning to burn through the open weave of the fine linen onto his skin. At least, that was how it felt. He checked his pocket for the marked banknotes he'd collected earlier from the police station. If all went according to plan, the notes would later be fingerprinted and produced as evidence.

"Car approaching," came a voice through his earpiece.

Jacques remained where he was. Back to the road, left foot resting on the bottom strut of the wooden fence at the boundary of the car parking space. The vehicle engine slowed, and the tyres scrunched on the rough gravel of the lay-by.

"Wait," he told himself. *One thousand, two thousand, three thousand,* he counted in his head. At the count of six thousand, Jacques turned. A battered and dusty Dacia pulled to a halt.

"Car a Dacia. Looks twenty years old at least. Foreign plates," Jacques whispered, knowing that the wire he was wearing would pick up the detail. He trusted that his colleagues would have noted the actual numbers and letters on the plates. The registration was probably already being checked through the central police system. He memorised the ID of the car anyway. It was habit. Useful. Just in case.

As the driver – the man he'd seen at the *kermesse* in Messandrierre and the Saturday market in Mende – got out of the vehicle, Jacques stood up straight and waited. Watching.

"*Bonjour*, Monsieur," the man said as he moved round to the back of the car and opened the boot.

"*Bonjour.*" Jacques pasted a broad smile across his face. "Do you have the little toy dog for my boy?"

The man nodded. "But it's sixty euros, Monsieur. I've had all the expense of bringing it here for you, and my colleague sold the one I had in stock before I could let him know that you wanted it." He smiled.

"Sixty euros! But we agreed forty."

"But they are very popular, Monsieur. And this is a toy Schnauzer puppy, Monsieur. Much more sought-after than the one you wanted." The man stood by the boot of the car, with the toy dog visible inside.

Jacques looked in. "Alright," he said. He reached into his pocket, pulled out the notes and held out the wodge of cash. "There you are."

"Thank you, Monsieur." The man pocketed the money and almost threw the toy at Jacques. As he made his way towards the front of the car, a police vehicle pulled out of the switchback junction. Jacques dropped the toy, followed the man, grabbed his left arm and pulled it back and up behind his back, pushing the vendor hard against the car.

"I think you might be under arrest, Monsieur," he said as Lefèvre arrived at Jacques' side and placed a hand on the vendor's shoulder.

"We'll take it from here, Jacques." Lefèvre, handcuffs at the ready, advised the man of his rights, and Jacques stepped back.

The deed done, Lefèvre nodded to Jacques.

Jacques walked back to his bike. Sitting astride the machine, he watched for a few moments as his old colleagues managed the business of the arrest, collecting the evidence and taking the man into custody. The parking area was empty again in a matter of minutes, and Jacques was alone.

Keys in the ignition, Jacques set the machine running. *And that still leaves me with a present to buy for Lucien's birthday.* Helmet on. He grinned.

"I suppose it will have to be a real puppy, after all." He put the bike in gear, and roared out on to the main road.

and then…

A heavy postern gate slammed shut behind a tall, broad-shouldered and muscled man. He swept his hand through his thick silver-grey hair and donned a black fedora. He glanced across at a waiting car, a silver Mercedes, and smiled. Striding out, he crossed the open space, moved towards the car, opened the passenger door and got in.

"I'll need a new name," he said.

glossary of terms

platane — tall, broad-canopied leafy tree used to create shade

aire — short for *aire de repos*, resting place or layby

le 29 mai — May 29th

enchanté — delighted to meet you

Jour de l'Ascension — Ascension Day, a holy day of obligation within the Catholic church that always falls on a Thursday

notaire — solicitor

lycée — secondary school

grand-père — grandfather

santé — cheers

papa — father or dad

comme-çi, comme-ça — like this or that

kermesse — fête

Père — Father in reference to a Catholic priest

canapés — small tasty bites served with drinks

pompiers	fire service
soutane	a long black garment worn by Catholic priests
À plus tard	later/until later
ferme	farm
Tour Eiffel	Eiffel Tower
Aubracs	honey-coloured cattle seen throughout the Cévennes
fromagerie	cheese stall
boulangerie	baker's stall
fête	gala
gendarme	policeman
Mairie	Town Hall
bonsoir	good evening
mon enfant	my child
mon fils	my son
bonjour	good morning/hello/goodbye
Nom	surname or family name
Point d'Interrogation	question mark
C&T œuvre d'art	chercher et trouver - search and find a work of art
allo	hello

avocat	barrister
crêche	day nursery for children and babies
coutelier	a cutler, trader who sells knives of all kinds
Carte d'Identité	Identity card
Toussaint	All Saints' Day, November 1st
salon	lounge
à demain	until tomorrow
police municipale	local police
arrondissement	administrative district in large cities
plan cadastral	equivalent of land registry
Le Drap d'Or	The Golden Cloth
entrées	starters
pain	bread
cornichons	gherkins
frites	fries
sauce au poivre	pepper sauce
iles flottantes	dessert of meringues in custard
pélardon	goat's cheese from the Cévennes
oui	yes

Garde Forestier	forest rangers
cafetière	coffee pot
c'est moi	it's me
capitainerie	port office
quai	quay or wharf
au revoir	see you soon
mama	Romanian for mother or mum
Duclos des flics	Duclos of the cops
Gilets Jaunes	Yellow Vests – refers to the body of ancillary workers in France who were protesting about pay and conditions
Ça va?	How are you?
apéritif	a pre-dinner drink
vide-grenier	jumble/yard/car boot sale
Privé	private
Entrez	Come in
Inspecteur	detective inspector

Fantastic Books
Great Authors

darkstroke is
an imprint of
Crooked Cat Books

- Gripping Thrillers
- Cosy Mysteries
- Romantic Chick-Lit
- Fascinating Historicals
- Exciting Fantasy
- Young Adult and Children's Adventures
- Non-Fiction

Discover us online
www.darkstroke.com

Find us on instagram:
www.instagram.com/darkstrokebooks

Printed in Great Britain
by Amazon